BOUND FOR MURDER

A HARDCOVER HOMICIDE

(A Juliet Page Cozy Mystery —Book One)

AUDREY SHINE

Audrey Shine

Audrey Shine is author of the JULIET PAGE COZY MYSTERY series, comprising five books (and counting).

Audrey would love to hear from you, so please visit www.audreyshineauthor.com to receive free ebooks, hear the latest news, and stay in touch.

BOOKS BY AUDREY SHINE

JULIET PAGE COZY MYSTERY

A HARDCOVER HOMICIDE (Book #1)

A LETHAL LEXICON (Book #2)

A VOLUME IN VENGEANCE (Book #3)

A TYPESET TRAGEDY (Book #4)

A FATAL FOOTNOTE (Book #5)

CHAPTER ONE

The book spines caught Juliet Page's eye, dusty and intriguing as she glimpsed them through the charity shop's dusty window. Old books? She couldn't help it. Immediately, she turned that way for a closer look.

The shop was on a narrow side street off the town's main road, but she had started detouring there regularly, because there was a green jacket in the clothing display that she loved.

She couldn't buy it, of course, because she'd never have an opportunity to wear such an outrageously glamorous garment. She always ended up spending long minutes standing indecisively in front of the clothing rail, before giving herself a firm talking-to, and turning away.

But books? That was a temptation she couldn't resist.

Someone had cleared out their attic or their basement, and dumped the contents in this humble little store in Oakridge, California. In that dusty pile, amid the well thumbed thrillers and shabby paperbacks, there might be a hidden gem, a rare book, even a sought after first edition. Excitement surged inside her as she pushed the door open.

The shop was warm, with the late summer sun glaring through the window, and the aircon valiantly, though ineffectively, rattling above it. Gripped in the throes of a heat wave, Oakridge was even hotter than it usually was in September.

Juliet barely noticed the stuffy heat. This could be the day she found what every rare book enthusiast dreamed of – a priceless discovery.

"Well, good morning!" the manager greeted her, alerted by the jingling of the old-fashioned bell. "You don't often come past at this time?"

"Good morning, Patsy," Juliet replied with a smile. Yup, her repeated sessions of staring at that green jacket had meant she was now on first-name terms with the manager, a very patient woman in her sixties, with silver-framed spectacles, who probably considered her nothing but a time-waster. "I'm on a three-week vacation starting today, so I decided to do some shopping."

"Oh, a vacation? That's nice! Going anywhere interesting?" Patsy asked.

"I was hoping to," Juliet admitted. "We were planning to go on an overseas trip somewhere, so I booked all my leave. But unfortunately, my husband has to work, so I'll be having a staycation."

"Well, Oakridge is lovely in September, isn't it? And you could always treat yourself to the jacket to make up for not going away?" Patsy asked, glancing in the direction of the rail.

Displayed on its hanger, the jacket's bright green, crushed velvet fabric had darker patchwork detail, and gold trim around the collar and cuffs. It was glorious, eye-catching, vivid. Everything she dreamed of wearing, but knew she didn't have the confidence to carry it off. And Mike, her husband, would roll his eyes incredulously if she brought home a garment like this.

"Is hippie style back in vogue?" he might say in an amused way. *"I hope you're not going to wear that to one of my work functions. I'll never get made partner if you do."*

Juliet sighed. "No, I haven't come in for the jacket this time," she admitted to Patsy.

"You know, it'll go perfectly with your hair color, and bring out your eyes," Patsy encouraged, gazing at Juliet's reddish-brown hair, which was thick and wavy, but which she usually kept tied back in a conservative ponytail.

Picking up the hanger, Patsy shook the jacket out, smoothing her hands down the velvet. "And it's medium, so it'll fit you like it's tailor-made. It'll bring out your beautiful skin, too."

"Maybe next time," Juliet said, blushing at the praise. In her mid-thirties, married for five years, she suddenly realized it had been a long time since she'd been called beautiful. "I actually came in today because I noticed you have a new shipment of books."

"Books? Ah, so you're a book lover?" Patsy replaced the coat on the rail. "Books fly out of here, but we had a big box donated yesterday from a donor who'd cleared out her mother's house. I've only just had time to set them out, so you get first pick. Hope you find something nice to read during your vacation!"

Eagerly, Juliet stepped forward.

"Just looking for something for yourself? Or for your kids?" Patsy asked helpfully.

Juliet didn't have kids. "I'm looking for something quite specific – a first edition, a collector's item."

"How interesting," Patsy said, sounding uncertain now about how to help, as if green jackets were more her area of expertise.

But Juliet knew what to look for. As a librarian at the Oakridge Public Library, she dealt with books all day. Of course, the ones that she bought into the library were all new, chosen carefully with the limited budget she had, but there were a few treasured pieces of history in the library itself, venerable older books, lovingly plastic-wrapped and cared for, that had brought joy, and opened new worlds, to hundreds of readers over the years.

Juliet always felt anxious when one of her special favorites was checked out by a member of the public. She hoped that they would not forget to return one of the irreplaceable, older books that the library might then lose forever.

Heading over to the charity shop display, she browsed quickly through it, keeping her eyes peeled for the rare treasure that she dreamed of finding, and picking up a few other books as she searched.

Mike didn't read much. As a busy lawyer whose ambition was to be made a partner at his firm, he didn't have time to read fiction, or anything really except his case histories and the news. But he had a small collection of graphic novels and there was one in excellent condition here.

It would be the perfect surprise for him, she decided. Mike had been quieter than usual lately, more withdrawn, less affectionate. Work pressure, he'd told her, but the gift of a book might cheer him up.

As she picked up the graphic novel, she saw what was underneath, buried out of sight in a pile that had been stacked on the shelf.

Gasping, Juliet felt goosebumps prickle her spine.

This was a first edition of the famous classic, Gulliver's Travels! The simplified kids' version of this famous tale had been one of her favorite childhood stories. The cover was white, the text gold-embossed, and it was clean and in remarkable condition for a book that had been printed more than a hundred years ago. Written by Jonathan Swift, this was an illustrated edition, which had been signed by the artist, Arthur Rackham.

What a find!

A first edition, with a signature, for only five dollars, ninety cents?

Juliet ran her fingers over the cover, reveling in the texture, feeling a sense of elation that this fine book would be hers. It was ludicrously underpriced. A book like this, she estimated, would be worth thousands of dollars to a collector. Not that she'd dream of selling it. To her, this book was priceless, a treasure to be kept, the first time she'd ever found such a hidden gem.

Picking up the book with the others she'd chosen, excitement bubbled inside her as she took her stash to the till.

"That'll be all for you?" Patsy asked.

"Yes." Gulping, but knowing she needed to be honest, Juliet asked, "This rare book? Are you sure the price is correct? It's in excellent condition and seems very underpriced."

The attendant glanced at the pile dubiously. Then she picked up the graphic novel and checked the label on the back.

"Looks fine," she nodded reassuringly.

"No, no," Juliet explained. "Not that one. *This* one. "Gulliver's Travels into Several Remote Nations of the World," she said in fond tones, placing her hand on the first edition's textured jacket.

"*That* old book?" Patsy asked in surprise.

"Oh, it's not just an old book! It's a first edition. This was published in the early 1900s."

"How do you know that?"

"You see here?" Picking up the book, Juliet cradled the spine in her palm, flipping it open carefully so as not to cause any damage. Gently, she turned to the copyright page. "You can see the date of publication here. And it says here, First Impression, so you know it's a first edition." The number below it begins with a 1, which is another clue."

"I see!" Patsy said, sounding intrigued.

"Look at the condition of the spine. The cover is hardly scuffed at all, and the pages are pristine," Juliet enthused, hoping that she wasn't being a bore, but her natural shyness was temporarily overridden by her passion for this topic.

Everyone should learn about the value of old books – there was so much history to be found in them. And they were irreplaceable. Once they were gone, they were gone.

"You're right! And the cover has a nice feel to it. Quality, with that gold lettering. Well, I've learned something today."

Juliet grinned in delight that Patsy had begun to share some of the enthusiasm that blazed inside her.

After Patsy rang up her purchases and put them in a paper bag. Juliet paid, grateful for the magical turn the day had taken. She'd found a treasure of a book, something of incredible value. Long ago, a publisher had proudly displayed it, a bookseller had stocked it, and a reader had loved it. And then, as time passed, it had been set aside and forgotten, growing dusty and neglected, until the big clear-out had set this book free to be appreciated again.

Feeling it was the right thing to do after acquiring a collector's item at such an amazing price, Juliet dug in her wallet, shoving all her loose dollars into the charity's tin, in support of an animal shelter.

Heading out, she decided that since she was only a couple of blocks away from Mike's offices, it would be the perfect opportunity to stop in and surprise him with the gift. She wouldn't stay long, of course, if he was very busy. But at least the graphic novel would brighten her husband's day.

And, if he had a few minutes to spare, perhaps he'd be ready to open up about what had been troubling him so much these past few weeks.

CHAPTER TWO

With her package under her arm, excitement still sizzling inside her, Juliet followed a route she knew well. Their downtown apartment was only a mile away from Mike's work, in one direction, and the Oakridge library, in the other.

She'd always joked that her handsome, sandy haired husband was just as married to his job as he was to her. He spent long hours at the law firm – hours that she had noticed had lengthened recently.

"I'll never be made partner if…" had become a familiar saying to Juliet over the past few years. She knew that her husband's career ambitions were his overriding concern right now. He was nearly forty, and if you didn't get made partner by forty at this law firm, apparently you never would.

That was why the overseas trip, which she'd been so looking forward to, had been shelved. She'd been gutted about that, but at the same time, she understood Mike's desperation to achieve this goal.

"I'll never be made partner if we take a long vacation now, Jules. Not with all these big cases on the go! It's all hands on deck from now until Christmas time."

Walking into the lobby of the law firm felt like entering another world – a sleek, professional, impersonal one. Heading across the marble tiles, she felt the temperature instantly plummet by thirty degrees. Compared to the furnace outside, it was slightly too chilly inside.

The receptionist in the lobby was busy with a call, ensconced behind her space-age desk, with a cool, blue wall behind her, a water feature, and ultra-realistic fake plants. Giving her a quick wave, Juliet headed to the elevator and up to the third floor, where Mike's office was located.

Juliet knew the drill. If Mike was in his office, he'd be available, and she could spend a few minutes with him. If he was in the meeting room on the opposite side of the corridor, then she'd have to leave the book with his secretary, Jess.

Jess was the latest in a series of smiling, platinum-haired paralegals who assisted Mike. Juliet guessed they all moved on to greater things because they never seemed to stay in that position for long. Jess had been there about six months, and Juliet always tried to be polite and friendly to her, though she sensed that Jess didn't like her particularly.

However, Jess wasn't at her desk in the small lobby outside Mike's office, where yet another fake plant was placed. Mike's office was spacious and well equipped, but not palatial, like the partners' offices on the fourth floor. Maybe they had real plants? Juliet had often wondered.

Jess's absence was strange for this time of the day. Juliet guessed she was out running errands. At any rate, it meant she didn't have to make forced, friendly conversation with Jess replying in monosyllables. And Mike must be available, because the meeting room opposite his office, was empty, the door open. What good timing!

Pleased that she'd be able to give him his book and hopefully have a chat, Juliet headed to the office door and tapped on it.

"Mike! Hey there! It's me!"

As she opened the door, Juliet heard a strange scuffling noise and a thud. There was just enough time for her to feel a jolt of surprise at what she'd heard before she pushed the door wider.

Aghast, she stared, feeling her world turn upside down.

Her husband wasn't at his desk. He was on the black leather couch opposite the window.

His shoes were lying on the carpet, one of them on its side. His tie was draped over the back of the visitor's chair, as if he'd flung it there.

His shirt was unbuttoned and his pants were unbuckled and there was a look of horror on his face.

Leaping off the couch, wildly groping for her plum-colored silk top, was Jess.

Her sweet, trilling voice was the one to breathlessly break the silence.

"Oh, Juliet – um – this isn't what it looks like!" Fumbling with her top, she pulled it on so fast there was the distinctive sound of a seam ripping. She gave Juliet a wobbly smile. Her cerise lipstick was smudged.

"Really?" Juliet said, clutching her package close to her chest, as if it was a life raft.

The word sounded faint and quivery. Emotions were storming within her. Shock, disbelief, followed by incredulity, and finally anger. The anger made her voice firmer.

“This isn’t what it looks like? Really? Then, please do explain what exactly it is?” she challenged Jess. The iciness in her voice surprised her, because inside, she felt like a collapsing wreck.

“You see, what happened is that I was, I was… aaargh!”

Jess’s imagination had clearly failed her at this critical time. Giving up on the explanation with a sob, she yanked her top straight, slotted her feet into her black, stiletto heeled shoes, and rushed out of the office at a teetering run, leaving a wave of sickly sweet perfume in her wake.

Mike’s face was crestfallen as he scrambled up off the couch and headed toward her, hands outstretched. Juliet flinched away. She didn’t want him to touch her now. Or ever.

“Juliet, why didn’t you wait before knocking?”

Those anguished words were the first thing out of his mouth. She stared at him in bafflement.

He was making this all her fault?

“Like waiting would have made it better? Are you telling me all you were interested in doing was hiding this from me?” Her voice rose to an uncharacteristic screech.

“That’s not what I meant! You’re misunderstanding me on purpose! We can talk about this. You know, there’s been fault on both sides. But we can’t discuss it when you’re so overemotional!”

Overemotional? He was definitely blaming this on her!

Now, the successions of platinum haired assistants, and all the late nights and working weekends, and the fact that Mike always put his smart, dress shirts straight in the washing machine when he got home, were starting to make sense.

If she'd smelled that perfume on his clothing or seen the smudges of lipstick like the one now visible on his collar, she'd have guessed the situation sooner.

Backing away from him, she spoke the words that sounded as if they were being uttered by an angry stranger.

“I don’t want to talk,” she said. “I’m leaving you. This marriage is over.”

“No, but Jules, seriously, we can try again…” Mike began, his face brick red.

Try again? What he was really telling her was that he wanted things his way, yet again. No way. Those times were done.

Recklessness surged inside her as she uttered the defiant words. “Unfortunately, I’m too busy. Tonight, I’m getting on an airplane. I’m going to go on that overseas vacation – all on my own.”

CHAPTER THREE

"Sarah? Sarah, you won't believe what I've just done!"

Juliet couldn't remember much of the walk home to the modern apartment that she and Mike shared. She'd called her older sister, who lived in San Francisco, as she was heading into the spare bedroom that was used as a storage room and a study. It was warm, small, and cluttered with furniture.

"You've – you've bought that lime green jacket from the charity store?" her sister guessed. "You've done that at last. I'm so proud of you. I need photos. Where are my photos?"

Slumping down on the office chair, Juliet could hear delighted barking in the background. She guessed her sis would just have gotten home from her half-day job as a doctor's receptionist, to an ecstatic reunion with her two rescue pups.

"No. Not that," Juliet said, gulping.

"Rusty! Bozo! Guys, I come home every day! Every day!" Sarah protested, as the barking reached a crescendo. Juliet could imagine the two pups leaping delightedly around her sister. Rusty, an Irish setter, had exactly the same hair color as her and her sis. Bozo was a spiky-haired terrier-type of unknown pedigree and dubious personality. He was an ankle biter who had to be locked in the bedroom when fast food was delivered. Sarah always said it was a good thing she loved him, because for sure, nobody else did.

"You'd think I'd been stranded on a desert island for a year. Yes, you're good boys. Very good boys. Sorry, Juliet. What *have* you done?"

"I'm leaving Mike," Juliet said in a small voice, suddenly feeling overwhelmed by the enormity of it all.

"My shoe!" Her sister's voice rose to a howl, as Juliet held the phone a few inches away from her ear. She didn't want to risk an eardrum rupture. "Which of you beautiful, naughty, terrible creatures chewed the heel off my shoe? That was my best pair of heels and I got it on sale!" Snorting in frustration, she lowered her voice again. "Sorry, sis. I didn't hear that properly. Did you say you were leading Mike?

Leading him where?" She sounded confused, as if her thoughts were going straight to collars and leashes.

"I'm leaving him! Leaving! I caught him on the couch in his office with his assistant!" Abruptly, Juliet found herself blinking tears away as she relived the excruciating moment.

There was a stunned silence.

"Oh, no! No! I don't believe it!" Shock was replaced by fury as Sarah growled, "You told me he said you couldn't go away on vacation because he was working too hard and he wouldn't be made partner if he took time off. Isn't that right?"

"That is what he told me," Juliet said, seething too.

"He said nothing about couch time! If he wasn't spending so much time on the couch, he'd probably *be* a partner by now! If I ever see that cheating scumbag again, and I mean *ever*…"

"You have carte blanche to do whatever you like," Juliet agreed, comforted by her sister's loyal support. "Well, whatever won't land you in jail," she corrected herself. Her sister was as tempestuous and reckless as Juliet was shy and reserved. No wonder she and Bozo got on so well.

"You're doing the right thing to leave," Sarah reassured her. "Mike will try to change your mind, though."

"I know. He's already called me five times. I haven't picked up, but I'm sure he's going to come home with flowers and apologies." Juliet felt her stomach churn at the thought. Flowers and apologies were not enough. She wanted out, because she had a nasty certainty this had been going on a while.

Why hadn't she seen the signs? They'd all been there, loud and clear.

All the times when she'd accepted his lateness at the office. All the times when he'd hung up on phone calls as she had walked in or turned his phone's screen away from her.

There had even been the time when she'd gathered up all her courage to ask him if he was sure everything was okay in their marriage, if anything was wrong, if there was anything he wanted to tell her. His blandly smiling reassurance that the distance between then was just due to work stress, had given her a massive sense of relief. *Premature* relief, as it turned out.

"You obviously are not going to be home when he gets back," Sarah said firmly. "Where are you going to go?"

Juliet sighed. "I told Mike I was going to take an overseas vacation on my own. I can't do that, of course. But at least I can spend some time moving out and finding somewhere else to stay. Somewhere with space for a rare book collection. I finally started my collection today, with an incredible find. The day was going so well, until it suddenly went wrong."

"But Juliet," Sarah said, in that voice she used when she was determined to have her way, "why *shouldn't* you go on an overseas vacation?"

"On my own?" she asked. "How can I do that?"

Sarah sounded patient as she replied. "Let me talk you through it. Firstly, you book the ticket. Then, you pack your clothes in a bag. Then you take a cab to the airport, remembering your passport. Pack your rare book, if you like, to read on the flight. Then you get on the airplane, and you –"

"Yes, yes, I know." Despite the circumstances, Juliet found herself laughing. "But all on my own?"

"There are plenty of places where solo travelers can have fun. How about – how about Tuscany? You could meet a dark haired, sad eyed Italian man who owns a winery, and you…"

"Right now, I don't want to meet *any* men," Juliet said firmly. "I don't think I should go anywhere. A sad eyed Italian is not a draw card at this moment."

"England," her sister said, equally firmly. "England is the perfect place. Loads of tourist sites, bed and breakfast hotels, you can travel practically anywhere by bus and train, and it's late summer. The ideal time to go. You should get at least one dry day." She laughed, as if amazed by her own wit.

"But I've been to London already. I went there on my honeymoon five years ago, remember? Mike and I did London and Paris. I don't want to go there again, not now."

"There is more to England than simply London," Sarah said authoritatively. "Go and explore the English countryside. Pick a village with a quirky name."

That rang a bell in Juliet's mind.

"I remember, in a book I read a while ago, there was a town called Whistling Willow. I always wondered if it was real," she admitted.

"Whistling Willow? It sounds like a joke name, but maybe it's real. If it is real, then why not? Why shouldn't you go there?

"I'm going to find out," Juliet said.

Her interest now piqued, Juliet looked it up online, not holding out much hope. Whistling Willow seemed like a name that would start and end between the covers of a children's fantasy book. Still, now was a good time to find out.

The screen refreshed, and she stared in surprise.

Whistling Willow was a real place. It was on the south side of the famous English Cotswolds, and it was a scenic riverside town. The photos that came up in her search looked postcard-perfect. Those rolling hills! Could grass really be *that* green? Or had they enhanced the color in the photograph? It looked impossibly bright and saturated.

Gazing at the stone cottages nestled in the curves of the hills, and the town's cobbled main street with bright flower pots lining the road, and the winding river, framed with willows, which widened into a small lake, Juliet was so captivated she forgot all about her marriage angst.

"It's a real place!" she said. "It's real – and it looks lovely."

"There you go, then!" Her sister paused. "You need to do this. You need to get away, get your head straight, and go somewhere where Mike can't change your mind."

"I'd love to go… maybe next week? After I've moved out?"

Steel was in Sarah's voice as she replied.

"If you don't do this now, you never will. I am going to give you a count of ten. I am going to count slowly, Juliet. And by the time I reach ten, you'd better be busy on the flight booking website. Or I am going to book it myself before I go out and walk the pups. And send you the ticket."

She'd do it, too. Her sister's threats were not to be taken lightly.

"One…" Sarah said inexorably. "Two. Three. Four. Five."

"Okay. I'm doing it! I'm doing it! I'll – I'll call you back when I'm done, okay?"

"I'll be waiting."

Gulping, feeling under pressure of time, Juliet clicked on the flight booking site, picking a date and a time, adrenaline surging as she confirmed her credit card details. Flights alone wouldn't be enough. She needed to get everything done. She clicked again, feeling a sense of unreality as new tabs opened. The bus ride from the airport – check. Accommodation in the first suitable place she could find – a lovely looking bed and breakfast. Check.

Finally, once everything was done, she called Sarah back.

"And?" her sister asked.

"I've done it!" Breathlessly, she announced her achievement. "I've just done the maddest thing I've ever done in my life. I fly this evening. This evening!"

Blood was pounding in her head. This was the kind of thing adventurous Sarah would do. Not shy, introverted Juliet. "I'd better start to pack!"

"There's one more thing you need to do," Sarah insisted.

"One more? What's that?" Juliet spoke over the whir of the printer as her black and white itinerary scrolled out of the machine.

"When you go to the airport, I need you to make a stop along the way."

"Where? To do what?"

"At that charity shop. You're picking up that green jacket you've been obsessing about." Satisfaction radiated from her sister's voice. "You're going to need something warm yet light when you get there. It's your chance to be different – and bright – and discover the new you, without Mike to worry about. In fact, I have a feeling that this trip and that jacket will be the start of a big change for you. You're going to have a huge adventure in Whistling Willow. I can feel it in my bones."

CHAPTER FOUR

"There you go. The Willow Guesthouse."

The cab driver stopped on the side of the narrow road and got out to open the trunk.

Scrambling out, Juliet stared around her, dizzy at the speed with which her environment had changed.

She felt heavy-eyed from tiredness, after a virtually sleepless overnight flight, followed by an Underground journey, then a change to a train. Finally, her exhausted mind was unable to interpret the bus schedule, which she seemed to have gotten wrong in her research, so she'd called a cab.

While in the cab, she'd divided her time between happily admiring the scenery outside, and feeling wretched and miserable while staring down at her wedding ring, which she hadn't yet taken off.

So many happy moments, so many hopes and dreams and plans, all had been woven into a marriage which was now frayed to nothing more than tattered memories. Really, she should take off the ring, but she didn't feel ready.

Now, here she was, standing on the side of the road, holding her bag as the cab drove off. The town looked even quainter and more picture book than it had done on her laptop. The main street was idyllic, with shop fronts discreetly signposted, wrought iron lamp posts with flower planters attached, and tiled roofs framing a gray-blue sky.

It was a cool day, with a hint of damp in the air, and a breeze that fluttered the Union Jack flag on its pole outside the guesthouse.

There were streams of tourists strolling down the cobbled street, dressed in colorful jackets, pausing at the shop windows, heading into the tearoom and the restaurant, taking selfies of the scenic view. A gray haired man in a tartan jacket, with a spaniel on a leash trotting alongside, must be a local. And that woman in the headscarf, filming him as he walked down the street, was definitely a tourist.

The smell of baking bread wafted up the road, fragrant in the damp air. It was coming from the tearoom, Juliet saw, a place selling bread and scones and Chelsea buns. Turning in the other direction, she saw the local pub on the edge of town, called the Willow and Whistle.

She stepped hurriedly back as a man on a bicycle whizzed past, clattering over the cobblestones. That near miss jerked her out of her reverie. Before she went exploring, she needed to check into the guesthouse.

The garden path, neatly paved in gray stone and bisecting a small, green lawn, led her up to the guesthouse. There, flower beds with a profusion of pink, yellow and white blossoms, lined the neat, stone house. She climbed up the three stairs, heaving her bag alongside.

An old-fashioned bell chimed as the door opened, and she stepped into the lobby. Squishy beige carpet covered the floor. A polished wooden table piled with papers served as a reception desk. There was a fireplace in the opposite wall that wasn't lit, but had wood stacked, and there were framed watercolors on the blue-wallpapered walls. Of course, Juliet noticed the bookshelf under the stairs, packed with books. From the spines, it looked like some were new, some elderly, and all well-read.

She took it all in for a moment, before footsteps on creaky floorboards clued her that someone was coming.

A woman about a head shorter than Juliet, with curly hair the color of cinnamon, bustled in, wiping her hands on her daisy-patterned apron.

Behind her, smaller footsteps sounded. Juliet watched in amusement as a large ginger tabby cat, wearing a blue collar, walked down the stairs behind the proprietor, headed to the reception desk, and jumped onto it.

"I'm Juliet Page," she introduced herself.

"Ah, Mrs. Page," the woman beamed. "Lovely to see you. Hope you had a good flight. It must've been a long day for you so far. We've got your room ready. It's upstairs, on the left. We've got some forms for you to fill in, which, of course, Gingerbread is now sitting on. Move, cat!"

She eased a clipboard off the desk and handed it to Juliet. "Let me take your bag."

"No, no," Juliet protested, looking at the steep wooden staircase, but the woman had already grasped the handle.

"I'm Mrs. Kildare. You come on up as soon as you've done the paperwork. Just put it back on the desk next to the cat."

Beaming at Juliet, Mrs. Kildare wheeled the bag to the stairs and hefted the bag nimbly up.

Juliet quickly scribbled her details on the form and replaced it on the desk. Gingerbread gave her a throaty meow, and she rubbed his soft head. That caused a rumbling purr to start up, so loud it filled the room.

She spent far longer than she'd planned to scratching his head, before turning away and climbing up the stairs herself. The treads creaked with every step, and the wooden stair rail, polished to a glowing sheen, felt slightly rickety. At the top, a white-painted door was open.

Beyond was her room.

A wooden wardrobe with a mirrored door was nestled in the far corner. The bed was sandwiched between the side wall and the sash window, which overlooked a well tended backyard, with terraced flowerbeds and a lemon tree.

It had a moss green coverlet, cream and yellow scatter cushions, and there was a vase of flowers on the small dressing table next to the bathroom door.

"You think it's alright?" Mrs. Kildare asked, tugging one of the yellow curtains straight.

Juliet stared around, entranced by the personal touches. There was a china teacup set on a tray with a tiny kettle and a glass jar of homemade cookies. On the wall was a painting of daisies, and the top shelf of the bookcase was lined with ornaments – a Friesian cow, a fluffy dog, a ginger cat.

Mike would have loved that Friesian cow. She could imagine him chortling at the goofy expression on its face. With that unwanted thought straying into her mind, her heart clenched at the sadness of this debacle and how different things had really been from the way she'd thought they were. If only time could rewind itself, and they could be happily married without the cheating.

Do *not* think of your soon-to-be-ex- husband, she told herself. Instead, she turned back to Mrs. Kildare.

"The room's gorgeous!" she replied.

"Well, dear, you let me know if there's anything else you need. We don't offer meals, seeing as how there are restaurants and a tearoom just a short stroll from here, but if you're peckish, and in need of a bite, we can always make you a sandwich."

Peckish! Now that was a lovely English word.

"Thank you," Juliet said.

"Meow!" Gingerbread said, strolling in and making a beeline for the bed.

Mrs. Kildare looked horrified. "Ginger! We don't go in guests' rooms! They might have asthma, or hayfever, or just – just not like cats!"

"It's fine," Juliet reassured her, feeling pleased that the cat had chosen her. "I love cats! If I leave the room, I'll make sure he goes out."

Gingerbread jumped on the bed and began kneading the coverlet with his paws, which were white, as if he'd trodden in milk.

Mrs. Kildare rolled her eyes. "As long as you're not troubled by him. He appeared a few months ago, skinny as a waif and yowling his head off. Got him to the vet, and he's healthy and well and neutered, but I really do need to find another home for him. I don't want guests to be worried by him, and he can be quite cheeky."

That was a shame, Juliet thought. Still, while she was here, she was happy to have a feline friend.

Mrs. Kildare paused at the door. Juliet thought she wanted to chat some more, but was weighing up whether she should, based on Juliet's appearance. Juliet guessed she looked even more tired than she felt, because, with another kind smile, Mrs. Kildare turned away and closed the door.

Juliet walked over to the bed and lowered herself down on it next to Gingerbread, staring at the ceiling, which had a decorative pattern pressed into it, and a lamp with a floral patterned lampshade.

"I'm here. I did it. I made it across the ocean."

"Meow," Gingerbread said, sounding approving.

She felt giddy with disbelief at being on the cusp of a two week adventure. Well, that was how long she'd booked her ticket for. It was flexible, and could be changed.

Far away from Oakridge, California, far away from her library job, and a good few thousand miles away from Mike.

A small part of Juliet's mind urged her to rest, to curl up and take a cat nap with Gingerbread, reminding her that she'd had a virtually sleepless night and that it was now already early afternoon.

She ignored that part. If she could make one impulsive decision, she could make more of the same. She was on a roll. Quickly, she unpacked, putting her clothes away in the wardrobe, and placing Gulliver's Travels on the top shelf. Yes, she'd brought her collector's item with her, carefully packaged in bubble wrap. How could she leave it behind?

With her book safely stashed, after a shower, and a change of clothes, she was heading out to explore.

***

Putting her knife down after slathering the last of the whipped cream onto her scone, Juliet lifted the crumbly chunk, and munched it appreciatively.

What a delightful, creamy, jammy, calorie filled treat that had been. Even the cup of tea – she'd chosen Earl Grey – was fragrant and perfect, totally in tune with the setting. Around her, the murmur of conversation and the clink of cutlery provided a comforting background ambiance.

"Well, did you enjoy that?" The tearoom's owner, who had a badge that read 'Amy Foster' came bustling over.

She had dark blond hair tied back in a ponytail and an efficient manner, but it was her beaming smile that made Juliet grin back in return.

"Best scone I've ever eaten," she said.

Amy winked conspiratorially. "There's a secret to the recipe that I can't reveal."

Juliet laughed. "I'm no baker. Even making toast is quite a challenge. Back home in California, I use my kitchen mostly for coffee."

Now, it was Amy's turn to snort with merriment. "Everyone can bake. Like everyone can cook. My old nan always used to say, if you can read, you can cook. Are you staying in town?"

"I'm here for two weeks," Juliet said, already wishing it was longer. Going back home, with so many memories waiting for her, felt like an unwelcome thought. She wanted to stay put, in this adventure, while her heart took time to heal.

Every time she thought of Mike, and her broken marriage, and all the memories that were not as happy now that her perspective had changed, it felt like a scab being ripped away.

"Come here again tomorrow," Amy said. "Tomorrow's my day for baking raspberry custard Danishes. They always sell out within a couple of hours. I could make triple quantities, but there's only so much baking a girl can do," she admitted. "But I'll save you one. And I'd love to have a chat about California. Would you be willing?" she asked, now looking anxious. "My young cousin's thinking of going to study at university in LA, and I'd love to know what it's like there."

"Of course I will," Juliet said, feeling glad she could help with some insider information. "The town where I live now is about a hundred miles south of LA, and I've been there many times. I even studied there for a year. How about tomorrow afternoon?"

"Sounds good. I look forward to it," Amy said gratefully.

Juliet paid with a ten pound note from the stash she'd drawn at the airport, and then picked up her purse and headed out.

The weather had changed, reminding her of Sarah's snarky comment about getting one dry day. It wasn't exactly raining, but the mist in the air had thickened and the clouds had lowered, making the bright shop windows even more enticing. Stepping out of the tearoom, she glanced across the street at the town hall, a modest building surrounded by a small border of grass, with two stone benches set in front of it. There was a large, printed notice on the wall notifying the public of upcoming events.

What events were taking place in this town hall? Curious, Juliet crossed the road to take a look.

"Well, this was worth it," she said, delighted by the range of activities that the town hall hosted.

On three separate weekday mornings, the Women's Guild met for knitting and sewing sessions. Juliet could imagine that no snippet of news or gossip about the wider area was ignored in those meetings. Then, there was the school play dress rehearsal, the Whistling Willow Agricultural Society's AGM, the Town Tourism Board's monthly meeting, an informative evening of Birds in the Cotswold Wilds for anyone interested, a Bingo evening (Seniors Free Entrance), and another senior event – an arts and crafts class.

And tonight, there was an auction of household and library contents, from the estate of Doctor Bill Townsend.

It felt like she was taking a peek into the real-life workings of the town. Despite the presence of the tourists, the list of activities gave Juliet a sense of the community life here.

"I must say," she murmured, "that household and library contents auction sounds interesting."

Perhaps there would be some hidden gems to be found. Although Juliet was sure that if there were, the bookstore down the road would snap them up.

As a librarian, she simply had to visit a bookstore on her first day in town, so after she'd finished reading the notice, Juliet headed that way.

Looking at the store's shop front, Juliet saw it was privately owned, not part of a chain, and its name was Willow Reads.

Willow reeds – willow reads? Aha! Her brain took a moment to get the pun. She was usually quicker with words, but nobody was at their best after two hours' sleep, she told herself.

Juliet felt eager to meet the owner of a private bookshop that had such a catchy name. Glancing at the window, she saw the wooden shelves were lined with bestsellers. Many of the famous American authors were proudly displayed at eye level. A few renowned British writers, too. Strangely, despite the creative name, the stock looked rather generic. But that might just be to entice customers through the doors. Perhaps there were old collector's items inside?

Glancing at the counter, she saw the attendant had her back turned, and was rummaging in one of the shelves.

She headed in, going straight to the back, to see what else might be there.

As she walked through the small store, she felt the way she always did when she was around books – happy and buoyant. She exchanged nods and smiles with a couple of customers who were browsing inside, scanning shelves that contained popular author names and new releases.

No collector's items? It didn't seem that this bookstore stocked older books at all. The only thing she found at the back of the store, practically hidden away in a dark corner, was a shelf labeled "*Local Cotswold Fiction*". Even this, it seemed, took second place to the international authors. If Juliet had run the store, she'd have put that shelf right up front. Surely all tourists wanted to buy something locally written?

Oh, well. Perhaps there was another bookstore in town that did things differently.

Selecting a new release at random from the row of thrillers – she was staying strictly away from romances for the time being – Juliet headed to the till.

There, a woman with a perfectly coiffed, rose gold hairstyle, red lipstick, and black-framed spectacles perched on the end of her aquiline nose, was busy serving a customer. She glanced at Juliet as she approached. Something about the sharpness of her gaze, combined with the stylishness of her appearance, made Juliet immediately conscious of her own ungroomed state. Hastily, she patted her hair, aware it was frizzy and it needed flat-ironing. She hadn't got any make-up on, and her sensible navy blue jacket had fluff on the collar.

Feeling self conscious, she sidled behind a bookshelf and waited for the man at the till to finish up. He looked to be in his late thirties, wearing a gray sweater with patches on the elbows. His dark hair looked slightly mussed from the back, and a couple of weeks overdue for a cut.

"Afternoon, Elizabeth," the man said.

"Afternoon, Oliver," the bookstore owner replied, giving him a winning smile. From this, Juliet deduced that they were both locals.

"How's business?" Oliver asked in a friendly way as she rang up his purchase.

"Never better," Elizabeth declared. Was she batting her eyelashes at him? She was certainly turning on the charm.

"Do you know what time the auction starts tonight?" he asked her conversationally.

She tossed her hair back before putting his book in a paper bag.

"No idea," she said. "You know old books don't interest me. My store focuses on the new releases."

Juliet cleared her throat, stepping forward and joining the conversation, hoping she wouldn't be intruding.

"It starts at six p.m.," she said shyly.

The dark-haired man turned to look at her. He had a pleasant face, with a mouth that quirked up at one corner, dark brown eyes with a sparkle to them, and a small scar on his right eyebrow. "Thank you so much. That's very useful information."

"It was on the notice, on the town hall door," she explained, making another futile attempt at patting down her hair.

He sighed. "On the notice, of course." His voice was rueful. "I didn't even think to look there. Thank you. That's very kind."

His smile was charming. Juliet had to admit, she found his English accent captivating. Suddenly, she felt better about her hair.

"It's a pleasure," she said.

He walked out, and Juliet stepped up to the till. Now that the gentleman in front of her had left, she saw that Elizabeth looked rather miffed. Her earlier charm had evaporated.

"That'll be all?" she asked Juliet, as if disappointed that she was buying only one book.

"Yes, thank you," Juliet said, taking out her wallet. Plucking up her courage to start a conversation with this rather intimidating woman, she took a deep breath.

"Are you the owner?"

"Yes, I am," she said. "I'm Elizabeth Mitchell."

"Your store has such a clever name," Juliet enthused.

"Well, I had to call it something topical." Elizabeth shrugged, clearly not as impressed by the compliment as Juliet had hoped she'd be.

"I'm Juliet Page, and I'm here on vacation. I'm a librarian back home in California," she said.

"That's nice."

Elizabeth held out her hand. Pleased that she'd gotten a personal introduction, Juliet held out hers, and shook it.

She withdrew her hand, but Elizabeth kept hers outstretched.

"Your credit card, please," she said in tones of forced patience.

"Oh, my *card*? Yes, of course." Her face flaming with embarrassment at having misinterpreted the woman's actions, Juliet rummaged in her purse for her card, and touched it to the machine.

"Do you stock any second-hand books? Any older, rare books?" she asked as she waited for the receipt to print.

Elizabeth shook her head. "I only do new," she said.

"Would dealing in second hand books not be a good business opportunity, with the local auctions in town, and so much history here?" Juliet asked. Her curiosity and enthusiasm were making her get ahead of herself.

Slamming the receipt down on the counter, Elizabeth tightened her lips, intensifying her glare.

"I've been a business owner here for years," she said icily. "I think I know the best way to run my business and what customers want. There are reams of second hand books in every bed and breakfast. Why should I stock them, too? New releases and famous authors are a guaranteed recipe for success."

The floor behind the desk was a little higher than the floor on Juliet's side, which made it even easier for Elizabeth to look down her nose at Juliet.

"Besides," she said, shoving the paper bag across the counter, "I stay away from those auctions. With the two collectors in town who are always at each other's throats, they're nothing but a recipe for disaster.

Things are going to explode during one of those auctions, and I don't want to be caught up in it."

CHAPTER FIVE

Should she? Or *shouldn't* she?

Juliet nibbled at her lower lip in indecision, while staring into the wooden wardrobe. She was all ready to head across the road to the auction – and feeling excited about the strong personalities who were likely to be there. There would be no shortage of local color tonight.

What about her own color choice, though?

"To each his fate, shaped by passion or sentiment," she muttered to herself, quoting a passage from Joseph Conrad, that often came to her mind in times of indecision. The words, though beautiful, were not helpful to her now in her decision-making.

Should she go for the flamboyant emerald green jacket, with its patchwork detail and sparkling gold trim? Or should she wear the trusty, conservative navy?

Juliet shook her head, feeling disappointed in herself as she reached for the navy jacket, and put it on.

"I'll wear you, I promise," she told the green jacket. "Just – just not tonight. It's an auction, after all. Better to dress in a quieter way at an auction."

She didn't even know why she said that. It wasn't even true. It was just her own shyness taking over, justifying why she didn't feel confident enough to flaunt such an eye-catching garment.

Feeling a mixture of shame and relief, she straightened the navy jacket's collar, completing her look – dark blue jeans, black boots, cream colored knit top. She'd finally managed to tame her hair, which was looking smooth and shiny.

A twinkle from her wedding finger caught her eye, and she stared down at the ring.

It could stay there, just for tonight, surely? Leaving it on would be easier. It would mean she didn't have to tug at that scab again.

No, she decided. It was wrong to keep wearing it. It felt like it didn't belong on her finger, or in her heart, any more. There was going to be no good moment to remove it. No perfect time. She'd just have to do it.

"You've already made the decision," she told herself.

It felt surprisingly tight. Getting it off her finger was a struggle. Twisting and wiggling, she finally managed to loosen it. Staring down at it, resting in the palm of her hand, she felt overwhelmed by the reality that she'd removed it.

She was going out tonight as a single woman.

The start of her new life. One that she'd never wanted, but which she was going to do her best to embrace.

"It has to be done," she said to Gingerbread, who was snoozing on the bed. He raised his head and looked at her wisely.

Picking up her purse, she put the ring in the inside zip-up pocket for safekeeping. Then, Juliet made sure she had her credit card in her wallet, just in case. Who knew if a rare find might pop up? The contents of a historic library might yield something significant, and she couldn't wait to find out what.

She picked up Gingerbread, who began to purr, feeling like a warm, furry sack in her arms. She'd have fluff all over the front of the navy jacket now. Serve her right for not choosing the green one, she thought. That would have been much more forgiving.

Putting Gingerbread down on the wooden floorboards, she closed the door and headed down the stairs, knowing already which stair was likely to offer the loudest creak.

Rain was pattering on the window.

"Weather's turned! Hope you're not going too far," Mrs. Kildare sang out, glancing into the lobby as she headed to the cozy living room beyond, carrying a tray with clean cups and saucers. "Rain's likely to worsen later. Might be wise to take a brolly from the basket by the door. Tomorrow's going to be fine, though."

"Thank you. I'm heading across the road to see the auction. I will take an umbrella," Juliet said. There was something about this English Cotswold rain that felt really wet. Much wetter than California rain.

She selected a black umbrella from the basket and opened it as soon as she was outside. Rain pattered down onto the canopy, and her shoe sloshed into a puddle as she headed across the cobblestones, glancing down the street to admire the sight of the twinkling lights. The stone frontages of the buildings, and the cobbled walkways, looked romantic and mysterious in the dim light.

Then, she stared in surprise at the activity coming from the town hall.

The large doors were open wide, with several doormats strategically placed on the tiled floor, to mop up the rain. Beyond, the town hall's lobby was light and bright, with people milling around inside. As she crossed the street, she heard music coming from inside, and the aroma of crisp pastry wafted toward her.

She wiped her feet on the doormats, folding her umbrella and shaking off the rain, and then stepped inside the lobby. The room, with its high, vaulted ceiling, might once have been a church, she guessed. Now, it was filled with bustling, laughing townsfolk all chatting to each other.

Mulled wine, cider, and sausage rolls were set out on a table on the right-hand side. Juliet gravitated over to the table, suddenly wishing she was here with somebody. The sociability of this occasion gave her a pang of loneliness.

She took a glass of cider, and munched on a sausage roll, with crispy pastry and soft, spicy filling. Delicious! The carbs made her feel comforted, as carbs always did.

As she turned away from the table, brushing sausage roll crumbs off her jacket's lapel, she nearly bumped right into a tall man.

"Sorry," she said automatically, moving aside. And then, glancing at his face, she realized she knew him. It was clearly mutual, because she saw the flash of recognition in the eyes of the man from the bookshop.

"Oh, it's you!" they both said together, as Juliet brushed more frantically at her crumbs. For some reason, she really wanted to be crumb-free right now.

"You kindly gave me the event's time earlier today. Thanks to you, I'm not late! I'm Oliver Cambridge," he said.

"I'm Juliet Page," she replied, with a smile. "Glad I could help."

Now, the crowds were gravitating from the lobby into the main hall. Carried along by the flow, they walked together.

"Are you here especially for the auction?" he asked. "Planning to bid?"

"No. I haven't even registered as a bidder. I'm in town on vacation," she said, twisting her hands together, aware of the empty place on her wedding finger where she was used to seeing, and feeling, the rings. "I happened to see the sign when I went exploring today and thought it sounded interesting." Juliet said.

"No shortage of interesting activities in this town, especially in tourist season," he agreed.

"Do you live here?" she asked.

"Yes, I do. I moved here three years ago." He frowned, the sparkle in his eyes suddenly muted, before continuing. "I'm a historian. I write schoolbooks, and locally based nonfiction, and I lecture to universities and schools."

"Lecturing? How fascinating!" Juliet said. She wondered if his move had been prompted by something sad. His expression had hinted at it, but the way he'd swiftly moved on told her he didn't want to talk about it. "This area must be so rich in history."

"It is. Do you know, just last week, when the town council was digging up one of the streets to lay a new water pipe, they found an exceptionally rare Roman coin? It was amazing." He checked himself as if not wanting to be a bore on a topic he was passionate about. "What do you do?"

"I'm a librarian," Juliet said humbly. "In a California town called Oakridge, about a hundred miles from LA." That was the best way of describing where she lived to a non-Californian.

"And are you traveling on your own?" he asked.

"I am." She felt her cheeks flush.

"Reason I was asking was – would you like to sit with me? I'd love some company. It should be quite interesting tonight, especially this first half, with the books on auction."

"That would be great. Thank you." They headed for the seating, and sat down on one of the long wooden benches. The hall was filling up fast. Juliet remembered what Elizabeth had said in the bookstore.

"I believe there's some rivalry between bidders?"

"Oh, yes." Oliver nodded wisely. Juliet took another sip of her cider as he stared around the hall, in a manner that told her he was searching for someone.

"There," he said. "You see the gray-bearded man with the trilby hat and the tweed jacket?"

Juliet spotted him immediately, sitting down in the front row. There was something entitled about his demeanor, she thought instantly. He was staring around as if he owned the place. Then he took out a leather covered journal and scribbled something in it decisively.

"Yes, I see him," she said.

"He's Alfred Douglas. He used to run an antiques shop in town, but he retired a couple of years ago and closed it. He's a wealth of information when it comes to local matters, so I deal with him fairly often, although he can be – difficult sometimes. He still collects items for his own enjoyment."

"How wonderful he's so passionate about what he does," Juliet said, but Oliver quirked an eyebrow.

"Unfortunately, Henry Wrexham – who's sitting down now, on the other side of the front row – doesn't think so."

Juliet craned her neck to see the man in a dark bomber jacket, with a neatly cut hairstyle and an aggressive tilt to his chin. He glared at Alfred before taking his seat, looking firmly ahead to the podium.

"And who's he?" she asked.

"Henry is the owner of a rival antique shop in a village a few miles north of here. He thought he'd had a big victory when Alfred closed his shop. It annoys him no end that some of the most valuable items still get snapped up by Alfred," Oliver said with a laugh.

Oliver really was a charming man, Juliet acknowledged. He had such an interesting way of telling a story. His dark eyes came to life when talking about the quirks of the townsfolk, and he looked at Juliet as if he was really seeing her. That was a special quality. As a librarian, she was used to being mostly invisible and blending into the background.

If she'd been looking for a vacation romance – well, of course, she wasn't. She had no interest in that at all. Nor did she know if Oliver had anyone special in his life. He seemed like he was single, but as bitter experience had recently taught Juliet, you couldn't always tell.

At that moment, the booming voice of the auctioneer interrupted their conversation. A hush filled the room as he adjusted his microphone.

"Ladies and gentlemen, welcome to tonight's auction, where some items from the Townsend Estate will be sold off. We'll start with the library contents, and then, after a short break, we'll move on to the furniture and other valuables. There are twenty items going under the hammer from the Heathway library, and we'll start with the first one. A set of ten Just William books, all first editions. Some loose pages and one jacket missing, otherwise condition is fair."

Juliet gasped, feeling her heart pound. The Just William books were children's classics. Who knew how many youngsters had fallen in love with reading, thanks to the captivating charm of these stories? And then first editions? That was going to fetch a sizeable sum. Her own fingers were twitching, even though she hadn't registered as a buyer, thanks to her unexpected meet-up with Oliver, and in any case, the price for this might end up being way beyond what she could afford.

"Who's offering me ten pounds for this prestigious collection?"

Ten immediately escalated to twenty, and then to thirty. Staring ahead in curiosity, Juliet saw that both Alfred and Henry were bidding on this must-have item.

"Fifty pounds? Do I have fifty pounds? How about sixty?"

It was war, Juliet saw. In between glaring at each other, both men were bidding aggressively, neither willing to back down. Honestly, she thought, this rivalry was every auctioneer's dream situation. Of course, it would make it impossible for somebody like her to win a bid. Both these men clearly knew their old books, and beating their rival was more important than getting a bargain.

"Aaand – we have two hundred and forty pounds. Going once, going twice – and sold to Mr. Douglas."

"Yes!" Oliver muttered, but Juliet was staring ahead, seeing Henry's angry glare as he turned to his rival, leaning across the seats as the people in between the two men pressed themselves back.

"You'd better back off for the next one!" Henry hissed. "I have a business to run!"

Juliet didn't hear Alfred's reply, but it sounded equally aggressive. Go to hell, said in a more genteel way, she summarized to herself.

"Order, please, order," the auctioneer said smoothly. "Quiet in the room as we move on to item two, a first edition of Tolstoy's War and Peace, in fair condition. There's a tea stain on one of the pages, and page 240 has been partially ripped."

The next book went to Henry, and the next one – a volume of classic poetry – was bought by a different collector, a woman with an elegant top-knot of gray hair and a twinkling diamond ring on her wedding hand – or rather, Juliet corrected herself in these circumstances, her *bidding* hand.

"That's Countess Claymore, who owns one of the local estates. She loves poetry," Oliver whispered.

Book followed book, the hammer thudded down again and again for increasingly large amounts, and only when the two adversaries decided not to bid, was it possible for anyone else to win.

"Now, we have the final item in this evening's books section," the auctioneer announced. There was a muted buzz in the air. This was going to be a sought-after item, Juliet knew, her arms prickling with anticipation.

"Charles Dickens' 'A Tale of Two Cities'," the auctioneer announced as Juliet's eyes widened. "A first edition classic, in mint condition. Undamaged and… signed by the author himself."

A collective sigh echoed around the room. Rustles and throat-clearings told Juliet that this book was going to attract a wider field of bidders. People had known about it, and come here especially to bid on it.

"We're starting at five hundred pounds. Who'll give me five hundred?"

Hands shot into the air. The bidding swiftly escalated. There was a stern looking man in a gray jacket and yellow tie, who'd bid on nothing else, but was now raising his hand in a businesslike fashion. There was the duchess who'd bid earlier, caught up in the excitement like everyone else. A few other people who looked like antique dealers started bidding, but dropped out as the price soared higher and higher. A thousand pounds. Two thousand. Five. Then ten.

It was breathlessly exciting to watch, but the air of competition was tangible. This was about more than just a valuable first edition, Juliet saw that clearly. This was about winning at all costs.

"Twenty thousand pounds?" The auctioneer raised his eyebrows at Henry, who thrust his hand aggressively into the air.

"Thirty thousand," Alfred called out, as gasps resounded around the room. He wasn't even waiting for the auctioneer, but escalating the bidding on his own.

"Forty," Henry shouted out.

"Fifty!" Alfred retorted.

Juliet had never seen anything like it. She felt a flash of sympathy for the snobbish Elizabeth. Now she understood why she'd decided to specialize in new books. There was simply no chance to acquire anything of value with these two rivals on the warpath.

The countess dropped out of the bidding, smiling and shaking her head. With an angry sigh, the gray suited man dropped out a few bids later. Now it was just Alfred and Henry, driving up the price in a room so filled with tension that Juliet expected the air to crack open.

"Ninety thousand pounds!" Alfred said decisively. There was a pause. Juliet saw more than one person gulp. Next to her, Oliver looked transfixed by the competition, his head turning from one man to the other.

"One hundred thousand pounds," Henry said, to loud gasps.

A hundred thousand pounds? Juliet felt her own heart racing. The stakes were sky high. This was a fortune to pay, even for such a special collector's item, but she reminded herself that money was nothing to some people, if it achieved their aims.

There was a ringing silence in the room.

"Going once," the auctioneer said. "Going twice." He raised his hammer.

Then, in a calm voice, Alfred said, "Two hundred thousand."

The auctioneer nearly lost his balance and fell right off the podium in shock. Gasps resounded around the room. Someone dropped their glass on the floor with a loud shattering sound.

Henry was glowering at Alfred, and Juliet realized, with a clench of her stomach, that this price was too high for him. He was an antiques dealer, not a private collector with a sizeable fortune to spend. Pride and ego aside, he had to make a business decision eventually.

He pressed his lips together, scowling at the floor as the auctioneer counted down once more.

"Going once… going twice… and sold to Mr. Douglas."

The room erupted into applause, with cheers and whistles resounding off the arched ceiling and breaking the tension that had held everyone still.

"A short break, ladies and gentlemen. Refresh your glasses before we move on to the household contents," the auctioneer said.

This seemed like the cue for a lot of people to leave, and a new group of bidders to start arriving. Standing up on wobbly legs, Juliet was wondering if this was enough excitement for one evening. All that tension had left her hungry. And thirsty, too.

"Shall we go and congratulate Alfred?" Oliver asked.

"That's a great idea. I'd love to meet him," Juliet enthused.

But, as they headed over to the crowd of people surrounding the lucky bidder, Juliet was nearly knocked off her feet as someone shouldered her aside.

Turning hurriedly, she saw it was Henry. The dark haired man was striding out of the hall with a face like thunder, bulldozing people out of his path.

It wasn't just the expression in his eyes that gave Juliet a flicker of worry as he passed. It was the words he muttered under his breath.

"He stole my book. That was mine for the taking! He's going to get what's coming to him."

CHAPTER SIX

Juliet's concern about Henry's anger was forgotten as she and Oliver reached the dapper, gray-bearded Alfred. Short, slim and spry, the collector was beaming in triumph as he held the prized book, which was now carefully wrapped.

"Well, Oliver, good evening to you! I'm very proud to have won that war, although I knew I would. Money's no object when it comes to valuable books, I always say. This is going to have pride of place in my extensive library," he bragged. Then his gaze fell on Juliet. "And who's your lady friend?"

"I'm Juliet Page," Juliet explained. "I'm a librarian, and I'm a huge fan of rare books. I have just started a collection – nothing as exciting as what you've just bought," she admitted, thinking of her treasured possession on the top shelf of the wardrobe.

"Really? You're a lover of rare books?" Alfred sounded more congenial as he shook her hand. "How wonderful you could attend this auction. I consider myself something of an expert in identifying the hidden gems that lurk in garage sales and jumble sales. However, when it comes to aggressive bidding, I'm even more of an expert."

"Charity shops have rare gems, too," Juliet said, remembering her find.

But it seemed that as well as having an unerring eye for quality, Alfred did love to dominate the conversation, because he didn't give Juliet a chance to say more than that.

"Yes. I feel that one has to have an educated eye when assessing a book. You know, in a few moments, one needs the knowledge to look at the condition of the spine, and the cover, and check if it's a real first edition."

"A real one?" Juliet asked.

"Oh, yes." Alfred frowned. "There are some remarkably good fakes out there, you know. And some bad ones, too. People will do anything when it comes to making money. I've been swindled a few times, by people who claimed I sold them a fake." Now, he looked furious.

"Really?" Juliet asked. She was disturbed by this. Fake books? It seemed that collecting was a more complex business than she'd thought.

"Oh, yes. I had to end up refunding them their money or losing my reputation," Alfred said. "But now, I keep a very close eye on my collection and I prefer not to sell. This book is for my own eyes and nobody else's. And I'll never sell it, although I know there are some who'd do anything to obtain it." His eyes gleamed.

"I'd love to learn more from you," Juliet said, wondering if he'd agree to share what he knew.

Even though she'd already figured out that Alfred could talk the hind leg off a donkey – to use an expression she remembered from a few English books she'd enjoyed – he obviously had a massive amount of knowledge. Telling a real book from a fake? She needed to know what the pointers were.

"Well, young lady, I'm never one to be parsimonious with knowledge, but I can see from your demeanor that you are a novice in the field, who needs a lot more education," he said.

"Absolutely," Juliet agreed humbly. Humility was the best response, because Alfred nodded.

"I can see you tomorrow – let's say, at two p.m. I'll be in the library of my home. We can have a cup of tea, and I'll educate you on what to look out for. I hope you know that this is an exception. I don't usually share my knowledge. However, you are a foreigner, and you asked nicely, and you caught me in a good mood."

He reached into his pocket and handed her a business card.

"Thank you so much," Juliet said. She put the card into the pocket of her sensible navy jacket, and she and Oliver said their goodbyes, making way for another wave of people offering their congratulations.

"I must apologize," Oliver muttered, as they walked away. "What Alfred said to you there was rather rude. I wanted to take him to task on it, but I thought that if I did, he might refuse to meet with you."

"I didn't mind the rudeness," Juliet said. There were times in the library when people were very rude, and as a public servant, she'd learned the best way to handle it was to ignore it and keep being polite. Rise above it. That was her motto. "If he explains what to look out for in a forgery, then it'll be more than worth it," she added.

"Are you going to watch the second half of the auction?" he asked, but although she was enjoying his company, she shook her head.

"I think I'm going to get some dinner now," Juliet said. She was starvingly hungry, and needed an early night. Now that the adrenaline of the auction was ebbing, she was realizing how tired she was.

"I wish I could offer to join you," Oliver said, in tones of genuine regret, as they headed back through the hall. "But there are a few historic items in the next half of the auction that I've been asked to give expert advice on. So I'll be assisting a couple of bidders."

"That's exciting," Juliet said. "I hope they end up getting their items for a better price than the Charles Dickens book."

She was about to turn away, when Oliver said, "Juliet, if – if you're not doing anything tomorrow, would you like to meet up for a coffee? Or even a scone?"

Even though Juliet definitely did not want any kind of romance, so hot on the heels of her marriage disaster, she couldn't help feeling a skip of her heart that she was going to see him again.

Remembering that she had promised to go back to the town's tea room to try Amy's raspberry custard Danish, she said, "How about the Scone and Cuppa, at four?" That should give her enough time after meeting with Alfred and learning more about rare books.

"That sounds excellent," Oliver said. "I'm looking forward to it."

"Me, too," she said.

She headed out of the town hall, together with knots of people – mostly locals, from their accents. Everyone was excitedly discussing the insane bidding war.

"Well exciting, wasn't it?" a blonde woman of about eighteen said to her friend, as they stopped off at the refreshments table for a final cider.

"That last bid just about did me in!" the friend confided.

Smiling, Juliet acknowledged how much fun it was to hear these colloquial expressions spoken with feeling, and not just read the words in books. It was lovely being here! She was so glad Sarah had persuaded her to travel.

Opening her umbrella to shield against the worsening rain, she decided that in this weather, the pub at the end of the town was too far away.

Instead, Juliet decided to try the small restaurant near the tearoom. It was already getting full, but there was a tiny corner table perfect for one. She sat down, ordered herself a glass of French white wine, and after a glance at the menu, decided to try the Irish stew.

As she sipped the wine and waited for her food, in the warm, comforting buzz of the restaurant, she felt her eyelids drooping, and hastily jerked herself upright. She didn't want to face plant on the table, and now that tiredness was catching up with her, there was a strong possibility she might. Forcing her eyes open, she felt relieved when the warm, steaming plate of stew arrived, with tender chunks of beef, carrots and potatoes – and Irish stout, according to the menu, which she couldn't taste, although the stew was deliciously rich and full of flavor.

But with every bite, the battle with her eyelids grew more intense. It was a fight she would willingly lose, since the warmth and comfort of the guesthouse was just a short walk away.

Eating the last forkful of delicious stew, Juliet called for the bill.

"What a day this has been," she muttered to herself as she waited to pay. She'd been too busy this afternoon to check her phone. Now, as she logged onto the restaurant's wifi, and glanced at the screen, she saw that Mike had messaged her no less than eight times.

Eight times?

Ire bubbled inside her, temporarily vanquishing the lure of sleep. Did he really think she was going to listen to what he had to say? Absolutely not! And she wasn't going to read the messages now.

She'd get back to Mike sometime, once she'd gotten the divorce under way. Until then, he could wait.

Juliet paid for the food and added a tip, not sure if the culture in Britain was the same as in the States, but wanting to rather err on the side of generosity. Then, she left, heading out into the rainy night.

Thanks to the downpour, the streets were a lot quieter now. Everyone had taken shelter in one of the restaurants, or the pub, or had gone home. She was alone, hurrying along in the pattering rain.

But then, she saw the couple ahead of her.

She actually heard them before she saw them. The woman's raised voice resounded angrily through the night, piercing through the spattering of rain on Juliet's umbrella.

This looked like a bad argument. Juliet immediately slowed. Her instinct was to avoid conflict. If this was a fight, she didn't want to get caught up in it.

Then again, what if it turned into domestic violence? She wouldn't turn away if that happened, and she would have to try to call somebody, or intervene.

Creeping forward and trying to observe without being seen, Juliet felt her shoes soaking up the bouncing droplets, while these two thrashed out what seemed to be a serious grudge.

It didn't look like a traditional couple, she realized, as she sidled past. The man, who had his back to her, was older, his hair gleaming silver, and the woman looked much younger, in her thirties, perhaps.

"You've done it again!" the woman shouted. "You're reckless and out of control. This is my future you're playing with! You don't care about anyone except yourself!"

"Your future? Do you really think you can control my life or have a say in how I spend my money?"

"I'm family! How can you even speak this way to me? You make everything about money and ego! This is not why I came here!" the woman lashed back, her voice shrill.

"Oh, please. Like you care about anyone but yourself?"

"Thankfully, that's not a trait I inherited," she replied. "I care about other people. I don't treat everyone like dirt! I've seen what you pay your staff, and it's disgusting!"

"Talking of money, I'll cut you out of my will, if that's your attitude! Give all the money to my brother instead. You know he doesn't have a penny to his name while I'm a successful self made man." The man's voice rose in fury.

"Uncle Basil is just as bad as you are. I will not let you do that!" Now, threat simmered in the woman's tone.

As she'd listened to this argument, Juliet had realized she knew who the speaker was. She'd recognized his voice, even though it was dark, and he was no longer wearing the trilby hat he'd sported for the auction.

The man having this bitter argument with a woman who must be his daughter, was none other than the famous local collector, Alfred Douglas himself.

CHAPTER SEVEN

A blaring noise roused Juliet from a deep slumber, yanking her out of a strange, intense dream where she'd been arguing with Charles Dickens himself over whether she could buy one of his handwritten manuscripts.

"But A Tale of Two Cities has a coffee stain on it, and a tear in the page," Dickens was protesting. "I mean, why would you want it, seeing as how it was the best of times, it was the worst of times?"

"I don't mind about the stain," Juliet pleaded, thinking that the bearded Dickens in her dream looked a lot like someone she'd recently met.

"I can't sell it with a stain! I'm going to use it to light fires," Dickens told her.

"No!" Juliet implored. "Please!"

Dickens began to laugh, a shrill, blaring noise that went on and on and on – until Juliet opened her eyes and found herself in the cozy semi-darkness of her guesthouse bedroom, with her phone shrilling on the nightstand.

She fumbled for it, hazy with sleep. If this was Mike, she was going to have a few choice words with him for having called her at seven a.m.

But it was Sarah.

"Hello, sis!" she answered, sounding groggy, clawing at her pillow and propping it against the brass headboard as she struggled into a sitting position. There was a strange, warm weight on her feet. Investigating further, she saw it was Gingerbread, sound asleep. She had no idea how he'd gotten in.

"Hello!" Sarah sounded bright and cheerful. "I did the math, and if I'm right, you're about to enjoy a pre-dinner drink? Hopefully you're at a pub somewhere?"

"You did the math wrong," Juliet said. "It's seven a.m. here. You woke me up!"

"Seven a.m.? No, that's impossible! You're six hours behind San Francisco, and I stayed up especially until eleven p.m. to call you!" Sarah sounded as confident as she did every time she made one of her spectacular math errors.

“England is not behind the States. It’s seven hours ahead, because of British summertime and daylight saving,” Juliet insisted tiredly. Math had never been her sister’s strong suit. English was. She was a sharp eyed editor, who worked for a publishing house.

“Are you sure?” Sarah sounded suspicious.

"Well, I'm here and in bed, and yes, I'm pretty sure it's morning," Juliet replied patiently.

There was a pause. “Oh, darn it. Yes, now I see where I went wrong. I subtracted instead of adding. How did I make that mistake?” Sarah sounded genuinely bemused.

“I know, I can’t believe it either.” There was a hint of sarcasm in Juliet’s voice. Sarah totally missed it, of course.

“So, are you having a good time?” Sarah asked.

“I’m having a wonderful time.” Feeling more awake now, Juliet scrambled out of bed and headed over to her mini tea and coffee station, snapping on the kettle. “I’m so glad you talked me into it. This town is fascinating and crammed with character. It’s unbelievably scenic. I’ve been to the local tearoom, and the restaurant, and the town hall. And the bookshop, of course.”

“Of course!” Sarah echoed.

“That was all I had time for. There was a rare book auction last night that I attended.”

She decided not to tell Sarah that she’d ended up sitting next to Oliver, or the warm feeling she had when she thought of seeing him today at the tearoom. She didn’t want her sister getting the wrong idea. Sarah would instantly jump to the wrong conclusion if she mentioned a man. Sarah was wedded to the idea of Juliet meeting a sad-eyed Italian who owned a winery. But a charming local historian, who seemed slightly shy, would be a close second runner.

“How awesome. Did you buy anything?”

“I didn’t have a chance. The bidding was insane. There were two local rivals who drove up the price of a first edition to crazy heights. It was hypnotic to watch.”

“You know, sis, talking to you…” Juliet realized that Sarah, who didn’t share her passion for older books, hadn’t really taken in a word she’d said. “Talking to you about your travels is making me dream of writing my novels all over again. I have this idea for a romance set in an English village. I’m thinking of a sad eyed bookseller, with a secret past. Do you think a sad eyed bookseller sounds like a character people would want to read about.”

"That sounds wonderful," Juliet agreed supportively. No sad eyed bookseller in this town. Only Elizabeth, who had a gimlet gaze and a distinct lack of charm.

Her sister's dream of writing a string of bestselling novels had been a dream for as long as Juliet could remember. The problem was that Sarah always gave up on the plot at around the third chapter. She'd started at least ten books, maybe more. And finished none of them.

But maybe the idyllic English village and the bookseller with a secret sorrow would prove to be the inspiration she needed.

"I'll take lots of photos and send them to you, to help you with your story," she promised.

"That'll be great!" Sarah's brain was now clearly racing ahead. "I'll give you a special thanks in the credits. I might even dedicate the book to you. 'This bestseller would not have been possible without the kind assistance of my younger sister.'"

"Well, I'll be glad to do any research you want," Juliet promised.

"I'm just so pleased you're there and that you're away from Mike. I know that it was so romantic when you met him, with him visiting the library to do case research, but honestly, I've never thought he was the man for you."

Now her sister was saying this? At the time would have been much more appropriate. Why had Sarah, who usually didn't have much filter, chosen to say nothing? Although caught up in the romance of meeting a handsome lawyer, Juliet acknowledged she might well not have listened.

"I'm thirty-three years old now and much wiser than I was back then. I have promised myself I'm going to choose better the next time," Juliet explained. "As Shakespeare put it, 'Love all, trust a few, do wrong to none.'"

"The bard says it best," Sarah agreed, but Juliet knew she was only humoring her. She was a much bigger Shakespeare fan than Sarah.

"And now, I'd better go."

"Back to sleep?" Sarah asked apologetically.

"That ship has sailed. I'm going to make some coffee and then go and explore the town some more. It's a beautiful day today."

Drawing the curtains back confirmed that fact. The sky was a pale blue, and she didn't see a cloud in it. The green hills of the countryside were visible beyond the cluster of gray roofs. How pretty!

A ray of sunshine spilled onto the bed, bathing Gingerbread in its glow. He rolled onto his back, stretching in ecstasy.

"So, you're sightseeing all day?"

"Not all day. In the afternoon, I have a meeting with a rare book collector who's going to explain to me how to spot a forgery. It's going to be very exciting. He's a rather egotistical man, but he said he's actually had incidents where he's been accused of selling forgeries himself," she said, turning her mind away from the scenic beauty.

"Sounds awesome, sis. Don't forget those pics! I must go too. Bozo and Milo are scratching at the door and telling me to come to bed!" With a giggle, Sarah hastily hung up.

That had been very sudden, Juliet mused. Could it be that her sister found any mention of rare books to be… boring?

Was that even *possible*?

Juliet pondered the question for a little while as she made her coffee. And it reminded her about the angry confrontation she'd overheard last night. He might be a local expert and the ex-owner of a successful antique shop, but it seemed that Alfred Douglas had a lot of conflicted relationships. She didn't want to get on the wrong side of him or offend him. She'd need to be very careful, Juliet decided. And she'd better get there early – just in case.

***

The cobbled pathway wound its way out of town, snaking in between the houses as it rose up the hill. Heading along it, looking out for Larkspur Road, Juliet checked the address yet again, and then checked time on her phone. The uphill walk had left her breathless. Alfred's house must be one of the bigger homes in town, set on the slopes of a hill, with a large garden.

It was exactly five to two, and she was now on the right road. His house must be the one ahead.

She was glad she was in time. Her morning had been spent in a relaxing way, walking around town, exploring some of the shops and alleyways near the guesthouse, with a visit to a bakery along the way – it seemed like the compulsory thing to do in this small town, because there had been a long queue for the sweet treats and savory delicacies.

Going up to Alfred's house, she'd then lingered on the slopes of the hillside, taking about twenty different photos for Sarah to admire and draw inspiration from. Then, she'd rushed the rest of the way, worried she'd end up being late.

But now, looking down at the town, and the country lane winding in between the houses, she took out her phone and snapped a few more shots, to capture the quiet ambiance.

The day was balmy, with a breeze ruffling the leaves of the oak trees that lined the gravel driveway as Juliet put away her phone and headed to the front door. From somewhere, the scent of freshly mown grass was wafting toward her. The house itself was a large, double story home, made of traditional Cotswold stone. On either side of the front door were clay pots filled with red geranium plants.

She wondered if Alfred would answer the door himself, or if he'd have a housekeeper or a maid. Well, she'd find out soon enough.

Raising the brass knocker, she brought it down, tapping lightly.

Then, she waited, puzzled by the silence.

Juliet was feeling conflicted now. Should she knock again? She remembered what Alfred had said last night. He'd told her that he would be in the library. Did that mean she was supposed to knock? Or that she should come right in and find the library?

Maybe he didn't want to have to walk all the way to the front door and let her in. Without appearing rude, she needed to decide on the best way forward, because now it was almost two p.m. And she really didn't want to be late.

Just in case, Juliet knocked once more, giving it a minute. Then, taking a deep breath and wishing she didn't have to walk into someone's house without them letting her in, she tried the door.

It was unlocked, which gave her a sense of relief. This must be what he'd meant her to do.

Stepping into the house, she took a moment for her eyes to adjust to the gloomy, cool interior as she turned to close the front door. She was standing in a paneled entrance hall with an antique table made from dark wood. On it stood a porcelain bowl filled with potpourri. The faint smell of the petals infused the still air. Everything was immaculate and polished, and there wasn't a speck of dust or dirt to be seen.

Now, where was the library?

"Um, Mr. Douglas?" she called out.

There was no answer that she could hear.

She hoped that he wouldn't consider her actions rude, but she seemed to be stuck in a rudeness dilemma. If she kept on knocking at the door, that would be rude. If she was late, that would be even ruder. And if she called him on the phone while she was standing in his entrance hall – well, this prickly man might consider that insufferably rude.

"Stop overthinking this," Juliet chastised herself. There was no need at all to act as if she'd burned her bridges when another few yards of walking might reveal the library, and Alfred himself. Perhaps he was slightly deaf.

There was the living room, with a glass paneled door. It was neat and tidy, and contained an elegant selection of antique furniture in dark wood, with rich blue and red upholstery. There was a room that looked to be a glassed-in porch. It was lined with plants and had wicker furniture. Perhaps this was what the English liked to call a conservatory.

Now, what was ahead? A wide staircase invited her to walk up, but she hesitated. Would the library be upstairs? She'd always understood that in these big houses, the communal rooms were on the first floor and the private rooms on the upper floor.

As she was standing, hesitant and nervous, a loud gonging noise made her jump so hard she almost dropped her purse.

A grandfather clock, around the corner from the stairs, was chiming two p.m. This meant she was late, and with every passing second, she was getting later.

Maybe the clock was positioned near the library?

Juliet hoped so. As she rushed around the corner, she saw the room she needed ahead of her. Tall shelves packed with books lined the walls. She'd found it. Thank goodness! And she was just in time.

Tapping on the open door, Juliet headed inside, treading on the plush carpet, which was a deep teal with white flecks. The bookcases towered majestically above her. The musty smell of paper and old binding filled the air.

"Mr. Douglas?"

There he was. Stepping cautiously into the room, she saw his feet. And his legs. They were visible from the leather wingback chair with its back to her.

Was he asleep? Her relief turned to worry as she headed in. Could he really be asleep, or might something more serious be the matter? Maybe he was ill?

"Mr. Douglas?" Concerned, she hurried closer.

He was in his chair, lying peacefully, as if asleep. His shiny shoes were planted on the floor. His hands were folded in his lap. The only thing out of place was the enormous dent in his head.

Juliet stared at it, gasping in a horrified breath, feeling as if her world had turned upside down for the second time in three days.

Alfred Douglas had been murdered.

CHAPTER EIGHT

Pacing up and down in the hallway, Juliet peeked through the open front door. She was shaking all over from shock at what she'd seen. A murder? In a town she'd firmly believed was the most peaceful place she'd ever been?

What was going on?

When she'd finally been able to think coherently again, she'd rushed out of the library, and then, out of the house. After some frantic research on her phone, she'd found the emergency number for the police. She'd called them, feeling exposed and scared. The killer might still be here somewhere!

But would he – or she – be in the house or the garden? In a state of high anxiety, she'd veered between the two, wondering which would be safer. Eventually, she'd compromised on a position just inside the front door, where she had a view of both. There didn't seem to be a soul around. Nobody else was in the house. And nobody else had passed by on the quiet road outside, until now.

The roar of an engine alerted her that someone was coming.

Heart speeding up again, she flung the door wide and stepped outside, relieved to see the blue and yellow shape of a police car, speeding up the hill.

It braked sharply outside, and the doors opened.

Two men climbed out. One was short and solid, with a broad face and a thatch of graying hair. The other was skinny and tall, with a stern expression, and looked about nineteen.

He couldn't be nineteen. Could he? Did they allow nineteen year olds to join the police?

The question swirled in Juliet's mind, illogically, as the men approached. Probably a distraction from the other, more serious questions, the ones she couldn't answer. Like: who on earth had done this?

"Good afternoon," the short policeman said in a perfunctory way, but his gaze was sharp and alert as he looked Juliet up and down. "I am Inspector Tennyson, this is Constable Coleridge, and I understand there's been a serious crime here?"

"Yes," she replied breathlessly. "Yes, there has. I arrived to see Mr. Alfred Douglas, who lives here, and found him – murdered."

The reality hit home to her as she spoke the words. Someone had murdered the wealthy man – arrogant and opinionated, but wise and knowledgeable.

"And you are?"

"I'm Juliet Page," she replied.

"Let's take a look." The inspector didn't head inside immediately, though. First, he opened his briefcase, pulled out a bag, and donned a pair of plastic foot covers. So did the constable. It made Juliet guiltily aware that she'd gone in there with no foot covers at all.

Inspector Tennyson pulled on a pair of gloves and then a head cover that looked like a shower cap. His constable did the same.

Only then did he grasp the front door handle that Juliet had touched roughly ten times, unthinkingly, during the past ten minutes.

"We'll need to get some fingerprints from that," he said, in a satisfied way.

Juliet gulped.

"I – um, I touched the door without knowing –" she began, but Inspector Tennyson was already striding inside.

"Show me where the body is," he said.

Thinking again of all that trace evidence, Juliet hovered by the door. "It's – it's down the passage, past the staircase, in the library straight ahead," she called.

She didn't want to go in there again. That had been a terrible sight. She'd never seen a dead body before, ever. It was impossible to think that someone could have come in there, with the most nefarious intent, and deliberately…

"No!" she said aloud, staring out at the sun-warmed village and the hills beyond.

After just a minute, she heard footsteps behind her and swung around. Inspector Tennyson was leading the way, looking brisk and motivated. Behind him was his taller shadow, Constable Coleridge, who literally hadn't said a word so far.

"Well," the inspector said, stopping at the front door and removing his gloves and foot covers. "This certainly is a murder. A brief examination of the downstairs rooms has shown us no sign of forced entry. Or of the murder weapon, which must have been a blunt object, used with some strength."

He gave Juliet an assessing stare. “How did you know the victim? What was your reason for being here this afternoon?”

Her stomach clenched. She didn’t think there could be anything worse than what had happened so far, but now, she realized that the inspector must suspect her. Of course! There hadn’t been another soul in sight. Obviously, though, a few words of explanation from her would set the situation straight.

“I was invited here. Mr. Douglas invited me yesterday, after the auction,” she said.

“The auction?”

“I met Mr. Douglas at the town hall, at an auction of rare books. He bid successfully on a few of the books.”

“Which ones?” He seemed interested, so Juliet was quick to explain.

“There was a set of Just William stories. He also bought a second edition of War and Peace, a first edition Dr. Seuss, a couple of first editions of poems, and a very expensive Charles Dickens first edition, A Tale of Two Cities. That caused a major bidding war,” Juliet remembered.

“It did?” The constable raised his eyebrows.

“Yes. It went for a massive sum of money, but it was in pristine condition. That’s the problem with old books, you know, they get read and handled and it causes damage. I guess that the owner of the deceased estate didn’t much care for Charles Dickens.”

She tried a joke to lighten the atmosphere because the inspector was looking at her strangely.

“You sound as if you know a lot about this subject?”

“I’m just an enthusiast who’s recently started collecting,” Juliet explained. “I’m here on vacation. I love old books and do know something about them. It's always been my dream to have rare, sought-after books on my shelf, and perhaps even do some buying and selling, start a little business –”

She stopped herself, realizing that she shouldn’t bore the police officer with her hopes and dreams. He had more important things to do, like finding a killer.

But Inspector Tennyson was looking at her strangely.

"I'm calling forensics here to go through this place for any trace evidence. And in the meantime, Ms. Page, I need to speak to you – in a formal interview, at the police station."

His tone contained a note of suspicion that made Juliet shiver.

He couldn't seriously think she was the killer. Or could he?

CHAPTER NINE

The police station was a side of Whistling Willow that Juliet hadn't yet seen. The small building was on the far side of the village square, which was seething with tourists. All of them turned to watch the fascinating sight of Juliet, accompanied by two policemen, clearly being escorted inside.

Red-faced, ducking her head, she hustled through the door. Nobody knew who she was, she told herself. They wouldn't remember her. Especially if she cooperated and didn't cause a scene.

Surely, in a few minutes, she'd be walking out again, with this unfortunate situation all cleared up?

The police station smelled of harsh cleaning products and warm vinyl seat covers. That was probably due to all the waiting chairs in the lobby, which were flooded with afternoon sunshine. She didn't get to sit there. Inspector Tennyson led her straight through to a small office beyond the lobby.

There was a cluttered desk with two chairs behind it. Inspector Tennyson went around the desk and sat down in a battered director's chair. Juliet took one of the seats on the other side, glancing nervously around at Constable Coleridge, who was standing by the door like a sentry.

"So, Ms. Page." The sight of the tape recorder on the desk did nothing to dispel her nerves. How had she ended up in a police station, being questioned – either as a suspect or a person of interest? She wasn't sure which, and neither was good. Glancing in the direction of Coleridge, the inspector ordered, "Take notes, please!"

"Yes, sir!" Constable Coleridge barked out, causing Juliet to jump violently. They were the first words he'd uttered! She'd begun to think he had some sort of special non-speaking role within the police.

"Ms. Page," the inspector continued. "Explain your exact movements since you arrived here."

"Well, it's my first full day here," she emphasized. "I arrived yesterday, mid afternoon. I checked into my guesthouse, and went and had a scone at the tearoom, and then found out about this auction. I attended it because I thought it sounded interesting. Since I'm a lover of old books, you understand? I met Mr. Douglas, he invited me to his home the next day, and I walked in and found him dead."

"Why did you just walk in?" the inspector challenged.

"Because nobody answered the door," Juliet explained. "He'd told me to meet him in the library, and I thought maybe I was supposed to go straight there."

"So you went there and found him dead?"

"That's correct. I…" It seemed wrong to speak badly of the dead, but she felt she needed to fully explain the situation. "I understand he did have a few enemies in the town. There was someone who was very angry about losing the bidding war, and later on, in the rain, I saw him having an argument with a woman in the street. I think she was his daughter."

But to her frustration, the inspector didn't seem that interested in her observations.

"Where is the book?"

"What book?' she asked.

"The book you told me about. A sale of two…" Hastily, referring to his notebook, the inspector corrected himself. "A Tale of Two Cities. You said that was the very expensive book that you saw him acquire yesterday?"

"That's correct. But I don't know where it is. How would I know?" she asked.

He tilted his head. "I see," he said enigmatically.

"Why do you ask?" She was feeling anxious now.

"I'll tell you where it isn't, Ms. Page." Coldness filled her as he continued. "It isn't with the other books that he acquired from that auction. All the other titles you mentioned were lined up on the small bookshelf just inside the library door. Clearly, that's the place that he uses to store his new purchases. And the Tale of Two Cities was nowhere. Was it, Constable?"

"No, sir!" Constable Coleridge yelled, causing Juliet to startle again, banging her knee on the edge of the desk in her fright. Couldn't he go for little and often, rather than these sudden, explosive outbursts?

"We sent another officer to do a search of the home, while waiting for forensics to arrive, while we took down your details and fingerprints," Inspector Tennyson said in pleased tones, as if proud of his on the spot research. "And although it is possible that the victim might have placed such a valuable item in a hidden safe which we have not yet found…" His gaze skewered Juliet. "It is also possible that this is a multiple crime. Not just murder, but robbery for profit. Robbery of a valuable item that the criminal knew about and perhaps intended to resell."

"It seems so," Juliet replied, trying to keep her voice steady. It was ridiculous that the inspector could even think she was guilty of this crime after just having arrived in town. She hadn't even known about the auction until last night. It was a shame that she couldn't account for her actions earlier, though, she realized with a pang. She'd been wandering innocently around town, peeking into the shops, sitting in the village green, and passing the time until her meeting.

It was doubtful anyone would remember her in her discreet navy jacket.

If she'd been wearing bright green, somebody might have noticed her. It was ironic to think her entire alibi might rest on a jacket she'd chosen not to wear.

"Your reason for attending this auction?"

"I was interested!"

"What job do you do, back in America?"

"I'm a librarian."

"Married? Single?"

She bristled at that question. What did it matter?

"In the process of a divorce. That's why I decided to take a vacation."

His face twitched. There was definitely some kind of reaction there, and Juliet wondered if this policeman was a victim of broken marriage himself. This wasn't the time to find out, though.

"So. you've got an interest in these collectable books, a dream of reselling them, you were at the auction last night, you were at Mr. Douglas's house today, and your fingerprints will probably be on all the door handles?"

"If I'd gone in to commit the crime, I wouldn't have left prints!" Juliet argued. Why was she even debating semantics with this stubborn officer.

"You might have committed a crime of passion. On the spot. Maybe you asked to buy the book and he refused. Right. Constable Coleridge?"

Juliet braced herself. But since no shout split the air from behind her, she guessed the constable must just have given an enthusiastic nod.

"Where's the blunt instrument then?" she demanded.

"The what?" the inspector frowned.

"The blunt instrument you said the killer used."

"Maybe I should be asking you that question." Propping his chin on his hands, the inspector gave her a narrow stare.

"I'm not the killer. And I have no idea where the blunt instrument might be." Juliet sighed. "This man had a lot of enemies. You'll find that out when you research him. For now, I was just in the right place at the right time – or rather, the wrong time. And I found his body."

She was amazed by the strength and confidence of her own words. And even the inspector looked partway convinced.

"We'll look into it," he said. "For now, though, you are a person of interest, and we'll need to speak to you again. You're staying in town, right?"

"For two weeks," she said.

"Keep your phone with you, and turned on. And if you need to go out of town for any reason, tell us." He glanced down at his notes. "I have your recorded address here, and we'll be sending an officer to search your room, so please do not return to your guesthouse for the next hour. Thank you, madam!"

That meant the interview was over, Juliet guessed. She got up, and headed out, on legs that felt shaky. She hadn't exactly been accused of murder or even had her passport seized. The police inspector hadn't gone that far, and she guessed that despite his intensive questioning, there was no actual evidence linking her to the crime.

She was sure he'd do the research, and find the killer, and that in a short time, she would be cleared. Not as yet, though. And if she was honest with herself, she had her doubts about the inspector. He didn't seem like the sharpest of investigators, along with his monosyllabic constable. Maybe he had hidden depths. Perhaps they both did. She sure hoped so.

As she stumbled up the road, Juliet felt as if she was walking in a dream, or rather a nightmare. She was so disoriented after what had happened this afternoon, that it was almost by accident she saw the hand painted, wooden sign of the tearoom ahead.

The tearoom!

Her raspberry custard Danish!

Her afternoon plans flooded back to her. They'd seemed so exciting at the time. Seeing the friendly Amy again, trying the bestselling sweet treat, and then having a cup of tea with Oliver.

Stress had driven them right out of her mind.

Unfortunately, after seeing the condition of Alfred Douglas's head, she didn't really feel in the mood for eating at all, still less anything containing raspberry. But a cup of tea? That, she could do.

And she'd need to break this terrible news to Oliver. He was a friend and business associate of the victim and would be horrified.

The tearoom was still bustling, but the early afternoon rush was over, and Juliet found a spare table just inside the door.

She slumped down, with troubling thoughts racing through her mind.

Who could have killed Alfred Douglas? It had been a targeted crime, with no sign of a break-in. He must have been relaxing in his chair when the killer had pounced.

He had many enemies. She'd seen confrontations between Alfred and two different people yesterday. Someone had hated him enough to kill him. Had the same person stolen the book? They must have left just before she had arrived.

But what would happen if the police dragged their feet on this? Alfred seemed to live alone, and he might not have any close friends.

Shivering, Juliet was reaching the uncomfortable conclusion that the person who knew most about the killer's possible identity might actually be – herself.

CHAPTER TEN

"Juliet! What's up?"

A cheerful voice interrupted her thoughts. It was Amy, the tearoom's owner, looking as upbeat as ever, her blond hair escaping from its ponytail to curl around her pink-cheeked face.

"The most terrible thing's just happened," Juliet said.

Amy's eyes widened.

"Wait!" she said, holding up a finger. "Before you say another word, just hang on a sec."

Juliet blinked as she turned away and rushed across the tearoom's tiled floor. A minute later, she was back with a steaming pot of tea, a jug of milk, a bowl of sugar lumps, and a couple of butter shortbread cookies on a saucer.

"Now, you can tell me," she said, sitting down opposite her. "We should have ten minutes to ourselves. The other tables are all fine for now. But you look like you've seen a ghost."

"Not a ghost exactly. But close enough." Lowering her voice, Juliet whispered, "Alfred Douglas asked me to meet him at his house at two p.m. He was going to tell me about rare books and forgeries. And when I got there, I found – well, I found he'd been murdered."

Amy blinked rapidly. "Alfred? Murdered?"

She didn't look quite as devastated as Juliet had expected her to. Her quizzical look resulted in a confession.

"That's terrible for you," she consoled her, pouring a cup of tea. "You must be so shocked. But I – well, perhaps I shouldn't go saying this now. I'm sure it's very insensitive. But he wasn't a nice man." She sighed, then continued in a near whisper. "He had such an ego that he'd come here and order tea and scones for himself and whoever he was trying to impress into selling him an old book, and he never used to pay."

"What?" Juliet asked incredulously. He'd bragged about being an aggressive bidder! Now, the words from that argument she'd overheard last night, about the way he treated people, were resonating in her mind.

Amy nodded. Her cheerful face couldn't quite do grim, but it looked like she was trying hard.

"He always said he would pay later, and with me being such a peacekeeper, I never wanted to embarrass him in front of his associates. You know, it's a problem, as a business owner in hospitality. If you accuse someone of not paying in public, it always ends up reflecting badly on you."

"But that's so wrong," Juliet said, feeling even more horrified. Alfred had been wealthy enough to buy a rare book for two hundred thousand pounds, but he hadn't paid his tearoom bills.

That was doubly shocking. Not only did it expose his character, but more worryingly, Juliet realized it made the list of people who could have killed him, much longer than it had been.

If he treated people so badly, there were going to be no shortage of motives for murder.

"I'm so sorry about that. It's appalling," she said.

"Well, I'm sorry you had to see such a thing," Amy sympathized. "How are you feeling?"

"It's the first dead body I've ever seen. It was a massive shock." Juliet admitted.

"You must sit here as long as you like," Amy said decisively. "And whatever you want to eat, it's on me. Although maybe you're not hungry. I guess - I guess you don't want a raspberry custard Danish now?"

Juliet took a deep breath. After an exhausting hour in the police interview room, the memory of the corpse was feeling a little more distant than it had done, and Amy's friendly face was seeming more real.

"You know what?" she said bravely. "I'd love to try one. I think some sugar will do me good right now."

"Let me get it for you," Amy said. She looked pleased to be able to help as she got up and bustled over to the kitchen, returning a moment later with a delicious-looking confectionery on a plate.

Juliet sliced a piece off, smelling the sweet vanilla of custard, overlaid by the tang of raspberry, and the buttery aroma of crispy, flaky pastry.

"It's excellent," she said after crunching down, pleased that she'd been able to try it, and was feeling a bit better after the earlier shock.

"Do they know who did it?" Amy asked.

"I don't think they have a clue," Juliet said. It was weird to be talking about such deadly matters, when in the background, there was the clink of teacups and the tinkling of cake forks on plates, and the sound of happy laughter. "Inspector Tennyson thinks I might have done it."

"You?" Amy's brow crinkled up. "How ridiculous. But then, he's a fairly useless inspector. I've always thought it's lucky this town has a low crime rate, because he's pretty hopeless at solving any crimes. He's a good inspector apart from that, of course."

"He is?" Juliet asked, taking another bite of the Danish.

"Well, you know, he does regular patrols, issues parking tickets, and he keeps the police station as neat as a pin, looks after the flower beds well. It's just the actual *solving* that seems to be a bit lacking."

"Hmmm," Juliet said. This was extremely worrying. She was a person of interest in a crime that was being solved by a detective with no talent for investigation.

A thought was occurring to her.

"You know, I personally already know of two people who could have killed him."

"You do?" Amy's eyes widened. Then, as if she had a spare set of eyes in the back of her head, she sprang up from her seat and rushed over to hand a departing table their bill. A moment later, after a quick check around her sweet-smelling domain, she was back.

"Two people?"

"Yes," Juliet said. She didn't want to say more. It might get her in trouble. Although she instinctively trusted Amy, she was the proprietor of a tearoom that was the hub of the town. Juliet was starting to realize that if she spoke about her suspicions, it might have consequences.

What if the real killer left town and did a runner, never to be seen again?

"I'm thinking it over, but I'm not ready to share what I think," Juliet said. Amy looked disappointed for a moment, as if she had hoped to get a big dollop of that juicy gossip. Then, she nodded wisely.

"Maybe you should tell the inspector. Help him along a bit?"

"I already did that," Juliet said slowly, although it was occurring to her that there might be a better idea, since he hadn't seemed to be listening. She wasn't sure of her idea's wisdom though. It seemed so daring, so reckless, so unlike her, that it needed time to crystallize in her brain.

“It might be wise to remind him,” Amy urged. “In case he loses focus and goes back to issuing parking tickets and giving warnings to the pub for staying open after hours.”

"I wouldn't want him to lose focus at all." Juliet's idea was gaining momentum now. It was starting to seem like it might be a viable idea. The only viable one, in fact. She had two weeks here. If this case wasn't solved in two weeks, she had a big problem. Would the inspector allow her to fly home? Would he seize her passport if he didn't find anyone else who might be the killer? It was all looking decidedly bleak.

Then, the tearoom door opened again, so loudly and suddenly that both their heads turned.

It was Oliver, looking stressed and traumatized, and without even needing him to say the words, Juliet knew that he’d already heard about the murder.

“Juliet!” he exclaimed, making a beeline for her table. “This is so awful. I’ve just received a call from the local museum owner. He said Alfred has been murdered – and that the police think an American woman might be involved in the crime. I – I don’t know what to say because I know you were supposed to see him earlier. Could they think it was you?”

Juliet felt her shoulders contract with stress. Trying to maintain a calm demeanor rather than collapse in a wretched heap, she nodded.

“I was the one who found the body.”

“No!” Oliver paled. “Are you – are you okay after that?”

“I’m feeling a little better now.” Bravely, Juliet took another forkful of the Danish. Truth be told, there wasn’t much bravery needed. It was delicious.

“You were there last night, when Alfred invited me to the meeting?”

“Yes, I was there.” Oliver nodded, sitting down at the table as Amy got up and rushed to get more refreshments. “I can confirm with the police that you went there because you were invited.”

“It would help if you could do that,” Juliet said, although she knew it might not put Inspector Tennyson off the trail. Inspector Tennyson seemed to think things had gone wrong at the meeting.

There was also the evidence, though – or the lack of it. “They’re searching my room, and they won’t find anything incriminating. I hope that clears me.”

“I hope so, too.” Oliver frowned. “I mean, you’re here to enjoy your vacation, and I’m sure you don’t want this hanging over your head, do you?”

“I can’t think of anything worse,” she admitted. “I feel so terrible about all of this. I came here as a vacationer, and now, I’m suddenly a suspected criminal!”

Amy returned, setting down a teacup and a few cookies in front of Oliver, who thanked her, before turning back to Juliet.

“The problem is that the book is missing,” she said. “That’s what makes it all so complicated.”

"The book he bid on?" Oliver sounded freshly horrified as he poured himself some tea and topped up Juliet's cup.

“Yes. The expensive one. The Charles Dickens first edition,” Juliet said. “All the other books he bid on were there. The police found them. That one has disappeared.”

"Robbery and murder?" Oliver spoke the words in a low voice. "I wonder if the original motive was robbery and the murder occurred as a result of it?" Then he caught himself, shaking his head. "I'm sorry. It's a macabre topic, and I'm sure you don't want to discuss it now."

"Actually, I don't mind discussing it now," Juliet said. "I feel like I need closure and to know that the killer's been caught. So I'm trying to remember anything and everything that might be helpful." She paused. "Now that I'm thinking about it, I would say he was murdered first, and then the book was taken."

"Why?" Oliver asked. "You don't think he tried to catch the criminal in the act and stop him or her?"

“He looked very peaceful, as if he was calm. I think whoever he was talking to, he was relaxed and confident. He was not fighting or struggling. They must have totally surprised him," Juliet said.

“That’s important to know. I guess the police will also have observed that,” Oliver said.

“I’m sure they will.” But this didn’t rule her out as the killer. There was no reason why, having invited her to his house, Alfred Douglas wouldn’t have been relaxed and confident when she arrived.

At any rate, that meant the killer had been someone he knew and had expected, or at any rate, not been surprised by. It wasn't a random book thief.

She saw the thoughtful expression on Oliver’s face, and knew that he was considering this problem deeply.

"You know, I have known Alfred for years," he said. "And I have to admit, though he's a knowledgeable man, he was also an extremely difficult man, very aggressive, and he made enemies easily."

"Yes, so I've heard," Juliet said, glancing in Amy's direction.

"A few times, I was shocked by how he treated people," Oliver mumbled, as if he felt bad speaking that way about a man who'd been murdered.

"It seems like there were a lot of people who might have wanted him dead," Juliet said, also in a low voice, because this did somehow seem like heresy. "After my dinner last night, I saw him having a vicious argument on the street, near a Land Rover that I guess was his?"

"That's the car he drives," Oliver agreed. "Who was he arguing with?"

"It was his daughter. At any rate, that was what it sounded like." Juliet wished she'd looked more closely now, but she had been trying to make herself invisible. "She was in her late twenties or early thirties, maybe? I remember her hair was light brown, and she wore a very smart white jacket, and she had a piercing voice." One other observation flitted back into her mind. "Oh, and she had a large, silver purse slung over her shoulder."

"That is really strange," Oliver said. "The description sounds a lot like Geraldine Douglas, and she has had a very difficult relationship with her father. It's well known in town."

Juliet felt shivers prickle her spine. If that historic conflict, late last night, had led to the murder, then this case could be closed, and her name cleared, within the hour.

"Tell me about it?" she asked.

"Everyone in Whistling Willow knows that ever since Geraldine was sixteen years old, she and her father have been fighting nonstop. Her mother passed away when she was very young. He tried to control her, she rebelled."

Expressively, he moved his hands to describe the repetitive and ongoing conflict.

"And then what happened?"

He shook his head. "A couple of years ago, she finally cut ties with him and moved out of Whistling Willow. I think she went all the way down south to Devon or Kent. I don't know if she's been back since."

There was a polite throat clearing from behind Oliver, and they both looked in that direction.

Amy stood there, looking slightly apologetic, holding a tray with an empty teacup on it.

"Please don't think I've been eavesdropping," she said, in a way that Juliet found just a little too earnest to be believable. "But I couldn't help hearing you mention Geraldine's name."

"Alfred's estranged daughter? Yes, we were discussing her," Oliver admitted.

"You know, I'll tell you something strange." Now, Amy dropped her voice, leaning closer. "I spotted her yesterday, in town, going into the grocery store. She was walking along with sunglasses and a headscarf on. I wasn't sure it was her until I heard her speak, and then it removed all doubt. All I could think was that she'd come back for a visit – but didn't want people to know."

Juliet stared at Oliver, aghast by this information.

And, at that moment, a portly form darkened the doorway of the tearoom.

Inspector Tennyson strode in, his face intent, heading straight for Juliet.

"Ms. Page," he announced. "We have some new information. Come with us, immediately!"

CHAPTER ELEVEN

Juliet gaped at the policeman.

New information? There was suspicion in his small, beady eyes as he stared at her. It made her feel strangely guilty, as if she might have sleepwalked and committed this crime, without knowing anything about it.

It was Oliver who said, with a frown, "Inspector, we've just been discussing this. There's no reason for Ms. Page to be under suspicion, just because she was a good citizen and she called you when she found a dead body? I was with her the night before, when she met Alfred Douglas. He invited her to learn about book forgeries, and she accepted the invitation. There was nothing sinister about it."

Juliet felt grateful that Oliver was in her corner, but she wasn't sure how much good his statement had done.

The inspector folded his arms, shaking his head slowly. Juliet noticed that the tearoom had gone quiet. The remaining customers were now drinking in this dramatic confrontation.

"We searched your room. Constable Coleridge has just reported back."

"Wait, he searched my guesthouse room?" Now, she felt herself reddening. The inspector had told her he'd do this when he'd interviewed her at the police station, but somehow, the reality of it was only hitting home now. She guessed she'd been too shocked earlier to take it in.

How far had this search gone? If she'd known a constable, who looked about nineteen and spoke in monosyllables, would have been rooting through her possessions, she'd have made a lot of different life decisions.

Starting with her choice of underwear. There were some shabby garments in that drawer. She'd packed for comfort, not for style. Her favorite bras and panties were uniformly plain, and all well worn, and one had a hole in it but she'd brought it anyway.

Her face felt on fire now. She was in the throes of a divorce! This wasn't exactly a romantic fortnight away. Juliet hadn't thought *anyone* would be looking through her underwear except for her.

The inspector didn't mention underwear, though. Instead, he said, "We found an old book in your possession, Ms. Page."

Her eyes widened. "But – *that* book? I know which one you mean, and it wasn't the Charles Dickens? It was one I bought at a charity store. I have no Charles Dickens first editions?"

"Nonetheless," he insisted, "it seems that you are an active collector, currently acquiring old volumes, and you therefore had a motive for the robbery, if not the murder. You might have come here especially for this auction, intending to bid on that famous book."

Juliet's pulse was pounding. She had to clear this situation up before it spiraled any further toward disaster.

"Gulliver's Travels is a book that I bought from a charity shop in California," she said. "I brought it with me because – because I didn't want to leave it behind."

"Why's that?" he asked.

Personal garments were yet again at the forefront of Juliet's mind as she realized she really did not want to air her dirty laundry in front of Oliver. However, there seemed no option. This policeman was putting her on the spot.

"Because," she said, now breathing hard. "Because straight after buying that book, I caught my husband cheating. I booked the flight to England the same day, which was the day before yesterday. I wanted to get some distance from him while I instigated divorce proceedings. I didn't want to leave such a special book behind. I am here for personal reasons and I didn't know about the auction!"

She was breathing hard, knowing that she'd provided all the tea room's residents with enough gossip to fuel them for a good few weeks. And now, Oliver knew her circumstances. He was looking sympathetically at her, but she hadn't wanted to spill her personal life out to him, and felt thoroughly embarrassed now. All she'd wanted was to be believed by the inspector.

"Well, that's a crying shame!"

The voice was Amy's. She was still hovering. Juliet realized that not much news escaped this tearoom owner, who clearly had hearing as sharp as a bat's. "You came here because of a traumatic life event, and now you're being harassed by the police, who can't understand why more than one person can own an old book?" She rolled her eyes.

"Inspector," Juliet said calmly, "everyone at the auction last night had an interest in old books. There were many collectors there. How about the rival bidder? Henry Wrexham? Surely he could have committed this crime?"

She didn't want to throw anyone under the bus, but for heaven's sake, the animosity between those two had been so tangible you could cut it with a knife.

Giving her a paternal smile, he shook his head.

"Those two have been rivals for years," he said. "Everyone in town knows about the healthy competition between them. I don't see why Mr. Wrexham would suddenly murder Mr. Douglas, after well over a decade of bidding wars."

That did cast some doubt, but she had another suggestion. It was time to repeat what she'd told the inspector earlier. Maybe this time he'd listen.

"Well, Alfred Douglas was having a terrible fight last night, in the street, with someone who I think might be his daughter."

"His daughter?" the inspector asked, surprised. "Geraldine moved out of Whistling Willow years ago. There's no daughter involved in this!"

He was going to any lengths not to suspect a local. That was the truth of it. This inspector was unwilling to believe that anyone who lived in Whistling Willow, or probably the wider Cotswold area, could be a killer. He was entrenched in his belief that locals were innocent.

"Well, I have nothing to do with this crime!" Juliet insisted.

"Nothing!" Amy echoed supportively.

"Nothing at all," Oliver said. "Ms. Page was only at the auction out of interest."

"And," Juliet concluded, "I I hope to goodness my old book is still in the condition in which you found it, and you haven't fingerprinted it!"

The inspector's gaze slid away, and Juliet began hyperventilating. Her precious collector's item, covered in fingerprint dust? It would take hours to clean. It might even need to be professionally restored after the police had finished with it! She hoped they hadn't damaged the spine.

"I accept your explanation," Inspector Tennyson said shortly. "There will be no reason to bring you in, since you've been prepared to give the information to me here."

And everyone else in the tearoom, she thought. Now, Oliver knew her circumstances. It wasn't that she would have hidden such information away, of course. It was just that – well, being a shy person, she tended to keep private information private. That was all. She'd have been more comfortable if he and Amy hadn't known. Now, they both did.

"I will speak to you later," the inspector said.

He turned and strode out.

Juliet waited nervously, in case he made a dramatic return and said he was bringing her in regardless – but after a few moments, the police car drove slowly away.

Gradually, the noise levels in the tearoom returned to their previous happy pitch, although one table, who'd paid the bill and were lingering, got up and left, looking as uncomfortable as Juliet felt.

"I'm so sorry to hear about your circumstances," Amy said. "That's just – well, terrible."

"I'm also very sorry." Oliver said. "And I think you did the right thing in getting away. Wiser to have a clean break, after something so damaging, that's affected your heart."

He touched his chest briefly, and looking at him, Juliet realized there was definitely a sorrowful look in his eyes. Had he, too, been through a divorce, or been cheated on? Something sad had happened to him, as he seemed to be speaking from personal experience.

"I'm glad you were both here to fend the inspector off," she said.

Giving her a conspiratorial wink, Amy turned and hurried away to clear a table, leaving Juliet to fret anew on her predicament.

Why on earth was the inspector so suspicious of her, just because she'd coincidentally arrived in town the day before, and attended the auction, and discovered the body, and had a rare book in her possession…

Reluctantly, Juliet acknowledged that there were quite a few reasons why the inspector might want to look at her more closely. Her recent history did seem to be interwoven with this crime.

But why wasn't he taking any notice of what she'd told him about the daughter? She'd handed him a lead on a plate, and he'd ignored it.

It might not be as easy as it seemed to figure out where Geraldine was, though, especially if she'd come to town with the intention of committing a crime.

Juliet caught herself.

What was she thinking? Was she actually thinking that she should go and hunt down Geraldine Douglas herself?

Yes. That was exactly what she was thinking. It couldn't hurt to ask a few questions – could it?

She stood up, intent on pursuing her risky but potentially rewarding endeavor. Only then did she catch Oliver's look of surprise.

"Are you heading out?"

Juliet thought quickly. "I just want to take a walk for a while. Alone. To get my head straight after all of this."

"Absolutely." He nodded.

"We'll speak soon," she said, seeing that he looked disappointed, but unwilling to tell him anything at all until she'd hunted down Geraldine. He'd tried to save her from trouble, and she didn't want to drag him into it.

Intent on her mission of discovery, Juliet turned and headed out.

CHAPTER TWELVE

Striding down the cobbled street, Juliet felt discouraged by the scope of the job she'd given herself. Hunting down a woman she'd seen once, in semi-darkness, in a town that was positively bursting with hotels, guesthouses, and Airbnbs?

What if Geraldine was staying in a neighboring town? That would make the search a thousand times harder. In fact, 'impossible' was the word she was seeking.

Maybe she should tell the inspector.

Briefly, she considered doing that, and then shook her head. Telling the inspector seemed like a pointless exercise. He didn't believe Geraldine was in town. Juliet did! She'd seen that fight with her own eyes, and Amy had corroborated the facts.

So, where would the aggressive daughter be?

As Juliet agonized over how, exactly, she was going to start her search, she heard her phone ringing in her pocket.

Thinking it would be the police, she pulled it out.

Letting her breath out in a long, frazzled sigh, she saw it was Mike calling.

Not for the first time. This was the third call she'd missed in quick succession. The background noise of the tearoom had drowned out her ringtone. She was in a dilemma now, because she couldn't turn her phone off, or even put it on silent. Not when the police might need to get hold of her at any time.

She could block Mike's number. Then she wouldn't be bothered by him anymore. Her lawyers would contact him soon enough.

But what if it was something urgent? What if the apartment had burned down, or Mike was seriously injured?

Dithering, Amy stared at the screen, her head telling her to block the number and her heart warning her that if something terrible did happen, she'd feel guilty.

She compromised by simply letting the call ring through to voicemail.

Then, deciding that she'd better let him know where she was and what she was going to be doing, she messaged him.

"I've gone overseas on a solo vacation. I don't want to speak to you right now. There's no way of resolving this, and I don't want to try. I'll brief my lawyer on the divorce arrangements, and I'll speak to you when I get back."

Juliet looked at the message in amazement. It was so – so harsh. So forthright and factual and terse. It wasn't the kind of message she usually sent.

Was she going to send it as it was? Or should she soften it a bit?

"No, no, no," she told herself firmly. "Next thing you'll be turning it into an apology note, knowing you! This is a time to stand up for yourself. You don't want incessant interruptions, and you don't want Mike on your back. Your situation is difficult enough without him complicating things too."

Taking a deep breath, she pressed the Send button.

It felt like a big step, to be asserting herself so strongly and laying down the law. A moment later, her phone buzzed again, this time with an incoming message.

Mike? Was he angrily replying and asking her why she was being so rude?

No, it wasn't Mike. To her relief, it was Sarah.

Hey, sis! Where are my pics? Keen to see your vacation town, and plan my bestseller!

Sarah didn't know how her world had turned topsy-turvy in the past few hours. And right then, Juliet didn't have the strength to explain.

Instead, she forwarded her sister all the scenic pics she'd taken from yesterday, on her walk up the hill. It made her shiver to think that she'd been in such a happy, innocent state of mind while snapping away. She hadn't known what awaited her at the top of the hill or how her life would change just a couple of minutes later.

"There you go!" she messaged, pretending lightheartedness even though her heart was lurking in the vicinity of her shoes. *"Can't wait to read Chapter 1!"*

And chapters two and three, she thought ruefully. That would probably be the point at which her sister's attention span faltered, and she gave it all up and started a new book.

Now, back to the hunt. How could she find Geraldine?

"You need to think logically," Juliet told herself as she strode along, her walk taking her in the direction of the local pub. She could see the sign in the growing darkness a couple of hundred yards away.

Logically, Geraldine would probably have stayed in this village, so that she could walk up to the house to do the deed. Driving up that quiet, narrow road would have been very obvious and conspicuous, and Amy had said she'd been wearing a headscarf and dark glasses, so she'd clearly been trying to stay inconspicuous.

Plus, Amy had seen her going into the grocery store. There would have been no reason for Geraldine to walk around in town, unless she was staying there.

"So, where would she be?" Sighing, Juliet tried to figure this out logically.

She'd never really considered herself a logical person, but now she thought about it, there was a lot of logic required in being a librarian. First of all, there was the book filing system itself. Complex and challenging, every book had to be correctly allocated and also correctly put away. Not an easy task. In a big library, a book that was misfiled could end up being lost for a good few months.

Then, there were the decisions on stocking and purchasing. Cold, hard logic had to be applied there, and emotions had to be firmly set aside when working with a strict budget. Many times, Juliet had let out a sorrowful gasp, knowing she was going to have to sacrifice her own personal favorites for the sake of what her library readers would prefer.

So, given that she applied logic during her working day, she could apply it now.

Geraldine was well dressed. She hadn't looked poor. That silver purse had not been a thrift store item. It had been dazzling, an accessory that had made Juliet think that if she were a different person, a more bold and adventurous type, she'd have lusted after it herself. Her shoes had also been stylish. More understated, but still expensive. It was interesting how the little details came back. Now, Juliet was surprised by how much she was able to remember.

So, given that she was wealthy, or at any rate, well off, Juliet didn't think she would have stayed somewhere cheap. It wouldn't be her style. She'd want somewhere with space, and a big mirror, so that she could check her reflection before going out, and store her expensive clothes and shoes in a well sized wardrobe.

Juliet felt pleased by how she was getting into Geraldine's mind.

"Then, there's the disguise," she said thoughtfully.

The disguise was important. That meant that Geraldine had not wanted to be recognized. And since this small town seemed to be a veritable hive of gossip, that would be difficult.

Anywhere small and local would have recognized her and the owners would have talked about it, just as Amy had done. Small, local accommodations were far more personal. The owners asked everything about you. They wanted to know, and they were curious, and they cared, just like Mrs. Kildare.

She sensed that Geraldine wouldn't have wanted that. Even the confrontation with her father had taken place in an empty street. Maybe she'd been waiting for her father to leave the auction, and spoken to him when she had seen he was alone.

Maybe she'd decided on the murder the next day. It was possible that Geraldine might not have come to Whistling Willow with the intention of killing him. She might have come to ask him for some money, or for a rare book to sell, or for some other reason, but ended up getting mad enough to kill him anyway.

The fact that she hadn't wanted to be recognized meant – impersonal.

Juliet slowed down her walk as she thought about this more carefully. Impersonal. That was what Geraldine would have wanted. A place where people saw you but didn't notice. Where they didn't care enough to talk.

That meant a bigger hotel chain. There were no large hotels in this town, but there were two medium sized places that were both part of chains, or franchises. Staying there would ensure a much higher level of anonymity. The staff would see a guest's name, but they wouldn't really care, and they wouldn't ask as many questions as a curious guesthouse owner.

So, the two hotels?

One was just a couple of hundred yards away. And one was all the way at the other end of town.

She was going to be doing a lot of walking, Juliet realized, unless she got lucky with the first hotel, or else managed to get the hourly bus that came through town.

She headed into the first of the chain hotels, realizing that the job of deduction had only gotten her partway. Now came the next challenge – seeing if she could find out if Geraldine was staying there.

There was only one way she could think of to do this, and that was to swan in with all the confidence in the world, and ask for her.

All the confidence in the world?

Juliet didn't have much confidence at the best of times. She'd need to pretend she did, though. A hotel receptionist would respond much better to a breezily confident request than to a mumbled, shy one.

Chin up, she marched into the hotel and headed over to the desk.

"Good afternoon," she said. "I'm here to see Geraldine Douglas. Could you call her for me, please?"

The receptionist looked puzzled. Then, she turned to her computer keyboard and began typing. Juliet watched her closely, looking for any signs of recognition in her eyes as she scanned the list.

She saw none.

"I'm afraid we don't have a guest of that name staying here," she said.

"Are you sure?" Juliet pretended forceful impatience. "She'd be about my height, light brown hair, or perhaps wearing a headscarf? With a silver purse?"

"I can't say from the description, ma'am, but we definitely don't have anyone of that name here."

Juliet nodded. "Oh, dear. Don't tell me I've misremembered the hotel?"

"A lot of people do that," the receptionist sympathized. "You'll probably find her in the one on the lower side of town."

"Thank you," Juliet said, marching out. She hoped the encounter would be entirely forgettable. Now, she'd need to repeat this all over again at the other hotel, and hope that she had better luck there. Otherwise, her theory could be ruled out as totally wrong.

At least she had some luck to start with. The bus was pulling up as she approached the stop. Running the last few yards and waving her hands frantically, Juliet managed to catch the driver's attention and jump on board. She slumped into a seat as the bus cruised through town, looking out of the window and admiring the view of the darkening evening, with pretty clusters of lights amid the hills, and a rising moon.

And then, the town was behind her and the last stop was ahead, with the double story hotel a little further down the road, its lights gleaming.

Scrambling to her feet, she got off the bus, and approached the hotel, hoping that this time, her story would yield results.

Heading into the lobby, she smelled a lemon-scented diffuser, and her feet trod on soft carpet. This was even more luxurious than the other hotel. Hopefully, that might improve the chances.

Striding up to the front desk, she gave a brisk smile.

"Good evening," she said. It seemed like a more appropriate greeting now that it was fully dark. "I have a meeting with Geraldine Douglas. Could you please call her?"

"Douglas, Douglas…" The blue uniformed receptionist, with her neatly tied back hair, stared intently at the computer screen, before picking up a phone and dialing. Juliet's heart leaped into her mouth.

Was she actually calling a room? Had her guess been right?

"Your name, ma'am?" she asked.

"Ms. Page," Juliet replied, using steely control to stop her voice from quivering with excitement.

What was she going to say if the receptionist called Geraldine down to the lobby? She needed to do some urgent thinking. She'd gotten lucky – or rather, her investigative skills had proven successful, she told herself.

Now to see if they could take her further, and get the truth out of Geraldine.

CHAPTER THIRTEEN

Juliet soon realized it wasn't going to be as easy as she thought.

The receptionist turned back to her, shaking her head regretfully. "Ma'am, Ms. Douglas is not in her room. She must have gone out."

"I'll wait for her, if that's alright," Juliet said.

"Of course. Please take a seat in the lobby."

Tension surged within her as she made her way to one of the blue-upholstered couches and sat down, watching the door. She'd found where Geraldine was staying and she was still booked in for the night, but she could be anywhere in town. This might be a long wait. But she had to try.

A waitress headed over and Juliet ordered coffee and, after some serious consideration, a slice of chocolate cake. She knew her diet in England so far was less than impressive health-wise. It had been practically nothing but carbs. Tomorrow, she promised herself, she'd have a healthy day, even if it meant avoiding the tearoom completely.

For now, though, sipping her coffee and digging her fork into the rich chocolate cake with its deep brown, glossy frosting, there was nothing to do except watch the door and hope that Geraldine would come back to the hotel before heading out for dinner.

Maybe she'd been setting up a false alibi, Juliet theorized. If she'd committed a murder in anger, that would be a sensible thing to do.

Or maybe she'd been meeting someone to sell the book she'd stolen.

Theories whirled in her mind as she waited, the minutes ticking past. A group of people in business suits walked in, heading to one of the conference rooms. A couple, carrying large suitcases, arrived to check in. A stressed looking mother dragged a recalcitrant toddler all the way across the lobby, his rebellious yells splitting the air.

And then, so suddenly that Juliet almost missed her, she saw a woman heading in.

She took her dark glasses off as she entered the lobby, and immediately, Juliet recognized her. This was Geraldine.

Nerves fizzed inside her as she jumped to her feet and headed toward her.

“Geraldine?” she blurted out.

The woman stopped in surprise, and turned her way.

For the first time, Juliet took her in properly – an attractive, strong-boned woman in her early forties, a little taller than her, and with the same bright blue eyes

However, Geraldine looked highly stressed. Her demeanor was rushed and anxious. Her mascara was smudged, and her light brown hair was messy.

“Who are you and what do you want?” she asked.

“I’m Juliet Page.”

Asking if she was a killer would not be the greatest start to this conversation. She needed to ease into this and not arouse the woman’s suspicion.

"I came here hoping to speak to you for a minute and ask a couple of questions. Could we sit down?" she asked, hoping this nonthreatening invitation would quell Geraldine's suspicions. She clearly had suspicions, and was glaring at Juliet in an adversarial way.

“I guess I can talk for a minute.”

“I’ve been waiting here, so shall we sit down? Coffee?” Juliet offered politely, leading the way to the group of chairs where she’d been sitting.

“I don’t drink coffee.” Geraldine plunked herself down in one of the armchairs and hooked the strap of her silver purse over the chair’s arm.

“Tea?”

“I don’t want tea.”

Juliet was running out of options. She did want to offer her some refreshment in exchange for her time – and for the stealthy chance to acquire information,

“Sparkling water?”

Geraldine glared at her in exasperation. “Are these the questions you wanted to ask?” she said sarcastically.

“No.” Deciding she’d better get to the point, Juliet gathered her courage. “I came here to ask you about your father.”

She didn't know what to expect when she dropped that bombshell.

Geraldine stared at her. Her face quivered, and her mouth twisted, and her nose twitched. Then, she began blinking furiously. And then, she burst into tears.

“It’s okay. It’s okay!” Frantically, Juliet signaled to the waitress for some water. She pushed her chair closer to Geraldine’s, and patted the hand that was tightly clamped around the chair’s padded arm.

“I’m so sorry. It must have been such a shock to you.”

What could she do but offer sympathy at such a traumatic time? Whether or not Geraldine had in fact killed her father, the fact remained that she was tearful about his death.

“It was a terrible shock. I – I can’t believe he’s gone. That he’s actually gone. I feel so bad,” Geraldine sobbed.

“Why’s that?” The water arrived, and Juliet slid a glass across the small, round table toward Geraldine, hoping that a sip or two of water would make her feel better.

“It’s because – because…” She picked up the glass and took a gulp.

Rummaging in her purse, Juliet found a tissue and passed that over, too. Then, she waited for Geraldine to finish what she was saying.

“It’s because I came here to try to smooth things over with him,” Geraldine admitted. “Why are you asking this, by the way?” Now there was a hint of suspicion in her voice, as her grief ebbed.

Juliet answered as truthfully as she could.

"I was just trying to piece things together for myself because I was the one who found his body. He was going to tell me about rare book forgeries. He invited me for a cup of tea.”

Geraldine sighed. “That was Dad for you. Always so generous with his knowledge, and always so damned impossible with anything else. He drove me mad, the way he treated people, like he took pleasure in being deliberately cruel.”

“It must have been difficult for you, being estranged?”

“Oh, you know about that, like everyone else in town? That’s exactly why I tried to come here without making a fuss. All I wanted to do was repair the relationship. Of course, it didn’t work out that way,” she said sourly.

“What went wrong?” Juliet asked.

"I had tea with him the day before yesterday. That seemed to go smoothly, and we managed not to fight. But there were still some things I wanted from him."

“What things?” Juliet asked, possible motives surging in her mind again.

“Private things,” Geraldine retorted.

“And when you tried to get them?”

"Oh, he was back to his old obnoxious self," she sighed, setting the water glass down and clasping her hands together. "All the way back to his worst. He'd just bid on a very expensive book, which didn't help. The timing was bad. He told me I must get in line and be an obedient daughter, and that I should appreciate him for who he was, and not ask him to do things like – like visit me every so often, and like calling my sister on her birthday, and all the things he doesn't bother to do because he's so darned important. And then he got insulting and I fought back and it turned into a disaster."

Juliet nodded sympathetically. She was getting the sense that the 'things' were parental, rather than financial. But Geraldine's evident anger could still have led her to murder.

"Did you try to see him again?" she asked.

"Well, I was going to call him today, and try one last time to sort things out. Goodness knows why, because any reasonable person would have given up. He's a stubborn man and won't change his ways. But I was out of town today on a prior engagement. A friend of mine in Oxford had a birthday lunch, so I drove there at eleven and only got back an hour ago. Of course, the afternoon was spoiled by the death. The police called, then half the damned town called, all telling me that he'd been killed. It was just so stressful! And I felt Dad and I had lost our chance forever."

"I'm so sorry things turned out that way," Juliet sympathized, realizing that this woman had just given her a solid alibi. If she'd been at a friend's birthday lunch, she could not possibly have killed him. "At least you know you did the right thing by trying to repair your relationship. Maybe he wasn't ready to do that?"

"And then, maybe it was too late," Geraldine said sadly.

Knowing now that her first suspect was innocent, Juliet wondered if she might still be able to get more information from her.

"Do you know who could have done such a thing?" she asked tentatively.

Geraldine shrugged. "No idea," she said. "No idea at all. If you ask me, it was a rival collector. He always used to brag about the books he obtained. Some of them for rock bottom prices, and others in bidding wars that went sky high. It was either one extreme or the other for him. Getting them was important to him."

"Who was his biggest rival?"

"Henry Wrexham, of course," Geraldine said. "But he'd brag to anyone. From his neighbors, to his friends, to fellow collectors – even

Uncle Basil, who's a right piece of work himself. There was nobody he wouldn't crow to about his achievements." Her face fell. "I can't believe I'm talking about him like this so soon after he's died. I think I have unresolved issues."

"Maybe you should speak to a therapist?" Juliet asked. But Geraldine shook her head.

"Not my style," she said. "I'll rather just bottle my feelings up and let them out in intermittently angry outbursts. That's what I'm comfortable with."

As she stood up, wiping her eyes with a sigh, Juliet wondered exactly how far the apple had fallen from the tree.

"I've got to go." Abruptly, and without another word, Geraldine strode away, leaving Juliet to call for the bill, and ponder what she'd learned.

She'd learned that Alfred Douglas liked to brag about his acquisitions. He would brag to whoever listened. And if they didn't listen, she strongly suspected he would make them listen. This man had a huge ego and it seemed that he had no filter whatsoever.

Bragging to fellow collectors?

What about the last straw that broke the camel's back?

Once again, she and Inspector Tennyson had different opinions. He thought that the rivalry between Alfred and Henry was just good natured competition, that had been going on for so long it could be discounted as a reason for murder.

Now, Juliet was thinking back again to the final, heart-pounding moments of that auction, as the book's price had soared sky high, and the tension in the room could be sliced with a blade.

She didn't think that had been a friendly rivalry, not at all.

Maybe that last, outrageous bid had finally cemented Henry's desire to destroy his rival forever.

CHAPTER FOURTEEN

“Henry Wrexham. Henry Wrexham, where do you live?”

Cross-legged on her bed, with Gingerbread watching her interestedly from the armchair, Juliet was scrolling through her phone, trying to do some on-the-spot research in her cozy bedroom.

Luckily, if Constable Coleridge had been through her clothing drawers, he'd left them tidy. Her book was missing, though, and she guessed it was now in police custody, smeared all over with silvery fingerprint dust. Maybe Inspector Tennyson had it on his desk, and was hoping it would end up being Exhibit A. Or maybe Exhibit B.

Her hope was that it wouldn't be an exhibit at all. And that she'd get it back as soon as possible when the real killer was in custody.

She cast her mind back to what Oliver had told her when they’d been sitting together at the auction. He’d said that Henry Wrexham ran an antique store in a neighboring town. That must mean he lived in the neighboring town, too? But which one. Could she find out by looking up his name?

Hoping she could, Juliet began her research. For a while, it didn’t seem to be getting her anywhere. Outside, she was aware that the background noise was quieter, and that from somewhere, delicious cooking smells were filtering into her room through the open window.

“Here we go!” The thought of dinner had been a motivator, because on the third page, her search yielded results. Here was an article on ‘the famous Henry Wrexham, antiques expert and lover of historical artifacts, whose beautiful boutique store is in the town of Finch.

Juliet scanned it, hoping to get more of a sense of the man himself from the printed words.

It was an in-depth interview, and the reporter had done a good job of capturing his essence, she thought. She'd asked him what his feelings were when he obtained a special piece, and he'd said, "It's the best feeling in the world. Nothing compares. For me, it's all about winning – not for myself, of course, but for my store, and my clients, who are all lovers of history and avid collectors."

Hmmm, Juliet thought, looking askance at the screen.

You're telling me you're cutthroat competitive, while trying to justify it by blaming your clients? That was what this piece hinted at. More than ever, she now saw what the loss of the Charles Dickens book, and the public humiliation of being annihilated by that massive counterbid, must have meant to this man.

The problem was, it was too late to go over to Finch now. The store would be closed, and she had no idea where he lived.

Her investigation would have to be put on ice until tomorrow. For now, it was time to go out and get some dinner.

As she put on her navy blue jacket and headed downstairs, Juliet wondered if she should ask Oliver to join her.

She'd really enjoyed his company. He'd been pleasant and charming. She was sure it hadn't been her imagination that he'd looked a little disappointed when she'd walked out of the tearoom alone?

And yet, she knew she wasn't ready for a new relationship, not even a holiday romance. It would be safer to steer clear of anything leading that way. Circumstances were complicated and her emotions were fragile, and she wanted to keep her distance from him, so that he didn't get the wrong idea.

Instead, Juliet decided, she should take positive action in her personal life. During dinner was the time to write an email to her lawyer friend, who she knew all the way back from school, and ask for his help in getting her divorce underway.

This time, she walked all the way back to the pub at the edge of town and headed in. The atmosphere was bright and cheerful, not the smoky den that she'd half expected. The pub was decked out in cream and royal blue, and it had paintings of farming on the walls. Sheep were being herded, apples were being picked, hay was being stacked. It was fairly full, and most of the customers seemed to be tourists, from the variety of accents she heard, as she made her way to one of the unoccupied tables.

"I'll have a glass of red wine, please," she said to the waiter.

"Small or large, ma'am?" he asked.

"Large," she said decisively. This was her divorce she was busy with.

She sipped it as she wrote the email, keeping it brief, but making sure she included everything she needed to.

"I caught Mike cheating," she wrote to Jackson, her university friend. *"I'm not interested in trying again. I want a clean break,*

according to the terms of the prenup. No fuss, no fighting, and as quick as possible. Can you organize for papers to be served?"

Looking at the email, she felt a sense of sadness.

It was her marriage. She'd had hopes and dreams for it. They'd been unsure about kids, deciding to keep that idea on ice for a while. They'd discussed getting a cat, but that had never materialized either. Mike had vetoed the idea, saying that when he was made partner, they could move to a house with a yard, and then get a cat.

The bigger house had never been bought. Their vacation had never happened. Even the partnership had never materialized. It felt, weirdly, as if the last five years had been a waste of time where her life was on pause, waiting for the impossible, because Mike's thoughts and his heart were elsewhere.

"It's time for me to live! Time for me to live at last, and make up for the lost years!" Juliet muttered to herself.

And, before she could think about what she was doing, she pulled out her phone, and Oliver's business card, and dialed his number with shaking hands, hoping that he'd be available and agree to join her.

Why should she dine alone when there was an option for charming and congenial company? And why should she turn her back on a new friend – who, she had to admit, made her heart flutter just a little?

***

Ten minutes later, Oliver walked into the pub. Juliet took a big breath, standing up as he wove his way to the table, and giving him a hug. The hug felt slightly awkward. It was as if they were both making sure not to get too close to each other.

"So," Oliver said, sitting down and signaling to the waiter for a beer, "you rushed out this afternoon, and I wondered if you had an idea about – about this whole debacle."

He gestured in a rather self-conscious way.

Juliet hesitated. She'd rushed into this clandestine investigation rather impulsively – and she wasn't used to acting recklessly at all. Would Oliver be upset if he knew what she was doing? English people could be sticklers for the rules.

But then again, he'd seemed firmly on her side, and it wasn't as if she'd been doing any official detective work. She'd just been asking questions.

“I was – I was…” Stumbling over the words, Juliet realized she still wasn’t sure about letting him all the way into her confidence. What if it ended up being a disaster? She’d trusted Mike. Look where that had gotten her!

“I was rushing back to my hotel room to message my sister,” she said, blushing, because she’d invited Oliver to dinner, and now, she wasn’t telling the truth about her day. She was leaving out a big, important chunk of it, and she felt bad about that.

Plus, she was turning crimson. She’d always been a terrible liar, and was already wishing she’d done things differently, but this situation was just too fragile to allow for her to take the leap.

“Your sister?” Luckily, Oliver didn’t notice her blush. “Where’s she?”

"She lives in San Francisco with two rescue dogs," Juliet explained. "After – well, after what you heard me say earlier, that whole – business, she was the one who persuaded me that I should travel here."

“I think that was a very good decision,” Oliver agreed with a grin that warmed Juliet more than she expected it to. His beer arrived, and Juliet quickly scanned the menu. After a glance at the options, she chose the Cotswold lamb curry.

“I’ll have the same,” Oliver said.

When the waiter had left, their conversation resumed.

“How do you feel about the area now?” Oliver asked. “You know, after the – the murder? I’m wondering if you want to go home, or travel somewhere else, now that this has happened?”

"Well, it's rather overwhelming," Juliet admitted. "I was so in love with the place when I arrived. Then this happened, and it was so shocking. But no, now you ask, it actually hasn't changed my opinion on the town. It'll be wonderful when it's solved, of course." Sooner rather than later, if I have anything to do with it, she thought. "And as for now, I've been advised by the police that I shouldn't travel too far. So I guess for the time being, I'm a local."

“A local? I always feel that’s the best way to travel. Admittedly, not when you’re caught up in something like this. But generally. I love staying in the smaller places, catching the local transport, eating at the places where the people in town eat. I used to do that with –” He stopped himself with a small shake of his head.

There was definitely something in his past he didn’t want to talk about. Now wasn’t the time to ask, so Juliet pretended she hadn’t heard that.

“I’m the same,” she admitted. “I love to become immersed in a place when I go there. And I’m feeling immersed in this place right now, despite what’s happened.”

Or maybe even because of it, she thought.

He gave her a rueful smile in which there was an appealing tinge of shyness.

She smiled right back, reminding herself that she had to keep her distance. She couldn't get too close to him. And she mustn't tell him what she was up to. Not until she knew him better and was sure she could trust him.

The moment was broken by their curries arriving, fragrant and rich and delicious, on beds of white, fluffy basmati rice.

As she dug her fork into the tasty food, Juliet reflected that the murder, tragic as it was, had allowed her to see a whole different side of the town. She’d met the local police. Kindness from strangers had been given so freely, and in fact, she thought of Amy and Oliver as friends now.

But what made it even more puzzling to Juliet was that she still didn’t think this was a town where a murder should have taken place. It felt completely out of sync, as if she’d arrived for a rare occurrence that would never happen again.

Maybe tomorrow it would all be solved. If her hunch was correct, then by lunchtime, the killer might be behind bars.

CHAPTER FIFTEEN

With flocks of butterflies flapping in her stomach, Juliet waited for the bus. This was going to be a make-or-break journey. She needed to have all her wits about her, because the police didn't believe in Henry Wrexham's guilt. She'd need to convince them, and that meant collecting strong evidence.

Or else some kind of admission to the crime.

As she was thinking frantically about what questions to ask, a sharp voice cut through her thoughts.

"Oh, it's you?"

She turned, to see Elizabeth Mitchell, the snobbish owner of the new bookstore, climbing out of a small, zippy looking red sports car. Elizabeth was dressed as stylishly as she'd been yesterday. Today, she sported a figure-hugging dress, in matte black, with a knee-length skirt and long, lace sleeves. Short, high heeled boots and a deep red coat slung over her shoulder, completed the ensemble.

"Good morning," Juliet replied, wishing that the bookstore owner hadn't made an appearance now. She didn't need any distractions when she was heading to such an important confrontation, and she had a strong feeling that Elizabeth didn't like her much.

"I wanted to ask you." Elizabeth sidled closer, her piercing blue eyes intent. "I heard from a client, who heard from somebody else, that you were escorted into the police station yesterday, accompanied by two detectives. The client distinctly said it was an auburn haired American woman, wearing a dull jacket." She rolled her eyes, as Juliet glanced self-consciously down at the navy jacket she'd picked yet again. "I know that there must be many Americans, conservatively dressed, in town at this time. But it did sound a lot like you?"

Her challenging stare convinced Juliet that she had heard all about the murder, and had also heard rumors that Juliet was somehow caught up in it.

This was very worrying. The whole town must know, and with the gossip flying around, it was probable that most people had found her guilty without even knowing who she was. Even Mrs. Kildare had carefully not spoken about the topic when Juliet had gone back to the guesthouse, simply mentioning in a sympathetic, yet reserved way, that the police had been in there earlier.

Suppressing the sense of panic that flared within her, Juliet raised her chin and stared firmly at the obnoxious bookstore owner.

"The police did speak to me," she said. "It was because Alfred invited me to tea, to discuss rare books and forgeries."

As she'd expected, Elizabeth wrinkled her nose when the term 'rare books' was mentioned.

"So, I was one of the first to find him."

Better not to say the actual first. Not to a woman who had an inexplicable grudge against her and seemed to want to bait her.

"That's not what I heard," Elizabeth said, a taunting note to her voice. "I heard something else, and it's surprising you're telling me such a different version."

Taking an angry breath, knowing that she needed to put this woman in her place, Juliet had no idea what she should say.

She was saved by the arrival of the bus, rolling smoothly around the corner and pulling up at the stop.

"See you later!" she said. "Have a nice day!"

That wasn't the response she'd wanted to give, but luckily, Elizabeth seemed even more miffed by Juliet's polite goodbye than she would have by the scathing response that Juliet had been groping for.

Tossing her hair back, she stalked down the road as Juliet clambered gratefully onto the bus. When she'd told Oliver last night that she loved the town, she should have included a disclaimer about the unlikeable bookstore owner.

Now, it was time to see if she could prove these rumors wrong.

***

Finch was as scenic as Whistling Willow. Climbing off the bus, Juliet saw the winding main street was lined with Cotswold stone buildings, and quaint shops, hanging baskets filled with flowers, and a village green surrounded by rowan trees.

Somehow, though, Juliet's heart was still in Whistling Willow. Maybe it was the quirky name or the fact that it had been the first Cotswold town she'd visited. Or maybe because she'd made friends there already.

In any case, Finch might be the home of a killer, she told herself, as she headed along the cobbled street. She'd waited to catch the eight-thirty morning bus, guessing that an antiques shop wouldn't open its doors too early. Now, at nine a.m., it was clear that most shops didn't open early. They were only starting to open their shutters and set out their street side tables now.

Juliet strolled past a bakery, fragrant with the aroma of loaves and pastries, and a clothing store that specialized in exactly the kind of quirky, colorful garments that she'd love to wear, but always felt scared to. She already had one bright green jacket languishing in the wardrobe. How much more stuff could she possibly buy that she'd never wear?

Quite a lot, it seemed, as she found herself detouring into the shop to buy the most gorgeous purse. Made from patchwork leather in tan, yellow, green and blue, with tassels on each side, it was bright and vivid and locally manufactured. Made by Cotswold artists, the label said! And her current purse was looking battered and worn.

In fact, there and then, Juliet transferred all her possessions into the new purse, and threw the old one into the next trash can she reached. This was her vacation, a time for change and excitement. The fact she was on the trail of a killer should not stop her from adding some color to her life.

With the new purse, soft and comfortable, slung over her shoulder, she continued up the road. The street reached a junction ahead, forking left and right. Reaching the junction, Juliet tried to figure out which way to turn. Left seemed to lead down to a lake, and the road was lined with restaurants and a few guesthouses.

Right seemed to be where the shops continued and where she guessed a destination antique store might be.

She headed up the road, discovering she was right. Here was the shop front she'd seen in the online article's photograph. In it, the smiling Henry, looking a lot more cheerful than he'd done at the auction, had been standing in front of a finely crafted signboard, on which was engraved "Cotswold Antiques".

Now, she was looking at that selfsame signboard. Below it, the shop's door was ajar, as if inviting customers in. The large window next to the door contained an intriguing selection of curios. There were some impressive items of furniture. A magnificent half-moon table in dark, polished wood, a rocking chair that looked a couple of centuries old, a plush armchair with red velvet upholstery. There was a pair of ornate vases on golden pedestals, an elegant white teapot and tray with pink rose designs, and a couple of paintings in heavy gold frames. The style made Juliet think of Monet. She loved that soft, romantic style, and had always vaguely disliked the stark, angular modern art that Mike had been so obsessed with.

There were also a couple of books in the window, leather-bound, with gold lettering on the spines, but she couldn't see more detail through the glass. Neither of them looked like the Charles Dickens book. Not that she expected to see it there. Displaying it in the window would not be a smart move. If Henry Wrexham had stolen it, he'd most likely made a clandestine sale to a private client.

Time to walk in and face the man himself.

Juliet took a deep breath. Then, she pushed open the door and headed inside.

Immediately, the musty smell of the place infused her nostrils. Not unpleasant, simply old. The smell of well cared for fabrics and upholstery that had seen centuries of use, with an undertone of the finest polish.

There were a lot of pieces crowding a relatively small space. Getting to the till felt like navigating a maze.

And there was Henry. He must have noticed her come in because the door had made a noise, but he didn't greet her until she was all the way at the front of the shop.

Then, he looked up from a leather-bound notebook he'd been writing in. With a pair of frameless spectacles on his nose and his hair neatly styled, he looked approachable rather than aggressive. He didn't look at all like the angry man who'd explosively made bid after bid before admitting defeat.

"Good morning, madam," he said politely. As he did so, she saw his gaze moving over her clothing in an assessing way. This was a man who was used to sizing up tourists and estimating their buying power. That was clear.

"Good morning," Juliet said politely. Now he knew she was an American, thanks to her accent, but he knew nothing else about her, and perhaps that gave her an advantage. It might be possible to work the conversation around to the deceased collector, and the missing book.

"What can I tempt you with?" His smile was positively charming. Looking at his eyes, though, she didn't see much warmth there.

"You've got such a wide selection here. It's so magnificent to see so many historic items under one roof," she enthused. The good thing about being an American tourist in a town like this, was that people expected her to enthuse. Difficult as it was for an introvert like herself to do it, at least he'd think it was normal. Perhaps he would respond by opening up and giving her some information.

He did. With a twinkle in his eye, he responded. "I have a passion for collecting the quality items of yesteryear. The joy of having a statement piece in your home is something that will last forever. There's no better way to remember the Cotswold area forever than by bringing a special treasure home, to remind you of this town, and England's heritage, every time you look at it. We do, of course, ship to America and handle the whole process," he said reassuringly.

Did he really think she was in the market for a five-figure antique table? Or was he just being polite, bolstering her ego just as she'd bolstered his? She didn't know, but now needed to steer the conversation around to those smaller, readable items.

"Actually, I'm a librarian back home," she said, and saw his expression instantly change as he recalibrated her buying power.

"How nice," he commented, his gaze drifting back to his leather-bound book.

"I'm passionate about old books," she said. "I've begun collecting."

"You have?" His gaze fixed on her once more, accompanied by a raised eyebrow.

"I love the old classics," she enthused, watching him carefully.

"You do?"

"Yes. My dream is to own a very famous first edition. You know, one of the ones by – say, Rudyard Kipling, or the Bronte sisters, or even Thackeray. Or Charles Dickens. A first edition of Charles Dickens would be a real find!"

His face darkened. "Well, in other circumstances, I should have been able to offer you that," he said.

"You should have?" Pretending innocence, she stared at him wide-eyed.

"I was cheated out of a collector's item that should have been mine by rights!" His voice rose, resounding around the room so sharply that she expected to see puffs of dust from the antique tapestries on the far wall.

"How terrible!" she sympathized.

"Yes," he said. "Terrible and pointless. You won't believe this." His voice suddenly lowered again. "But the man who cheated me was murdered yesterday – and the book that he stole from me is now missing!"

"I don't believe it!" Juliet made sure to look shocked.

"It's the truth, I tell you," he muttered, his charming smile replaced by an angry grimace.

"Who could have done such a thing?" she asked.

"I know." He narrowed his eyes, staring beyond her.

"If you know, don't you think you should – tell somebody?" she tried.

"I don't grass on people," he said. It took her a moment to work out the terminology, her brain delving into the memories of her British reading pile. Americans would have said 'I'm no snitch'. But the meaning was the same. He was hinting to her that he knew who'd done it. Was he telling the truth? She didn't know. It seemed like he'd veered into the realms of imagination.

"I'd be so interested to know who would do such a thing," she said brightly, trying again, but his gaze was still fixed on what was behind her.

Was there something behind her?

Glancing around, Juliet felt her heart leap into her throat. The store's door had opened again, and light was flooding in, making the dust motes dance.

The tall, lanky form of Constable Coleridge was silhouetted against the brightness. And she knew, with a thud of her heart, that the shorter Inspector Tennyson would be in front of him.

The police were here? Finally, they'd decided to question the antique dealer accused of 'friendly rivalry'. At the worst possible time!

"Police!" The word rang out, sharp and authoritative, as Inspector Tennyson's broad frame advanced.

She didn't want to bump into Inspector Tennyson again, particularly not while on a suspect's premises, in a place that displayed antiques. He might leap to the wrong conclusion about her all over again. It would be far better to stay under his radar.

She needed to discreetly leave as fast as she could. Was there an alternative route out of here, through all this furniture? If not, she was going to make one!

Ducking aside, she zigzagged to the side of the shop, seeing an ornate wardrobe there. There was enough space to squeeze behind it until the police were focused on Mr. Wrexham. Then, she could quietly sneak out.

As he approached the counter, Inspector Tennyson spoke in a stern tone – but not as stern as the one he'd used for her, Juliet decided.

There was a note of deference to it now, a 'sorry to trouble you' attitude that must be because he was a local.

"Mr. Wrexham? Inspector Tennyson and Constable Coleridge. We need to have a word, if you don't mind?"

"Of course not, sirs." The antique dealer's tone was now awash with courtesy. Already, he was oozing charm, presenting himself as a blameless local businessman.

Now they were all engaged in conversation together, she could leave without being noticed.

But then, as she was about to head briskly for the door, a little voice spoke calmly in her head.

"If you stay here," the voice said, *"you'll hear what Henry Wrexham has to say. That could prove useful."*

Gathering her courage, Juliet resolved to stay in hiding behind the wardrobe.

She might overhear something important and valuable. Hoping this would happen, she held her breath and listened.

CHAPTER SIXTEEN

"I'm very sorry to interrupt you during your working day," Inspector Tennyson began the conversation with the antique dealer, as Juliet tried to imitate the Greek statue in the corner of the room.

In terms of stillness, at least. Not in terms of the actual pose. The statue had one arm up and he was naked, whereas she had both arms pressed to her sides, and tension was causing her to perspire under her knit top and sensible jacket. If she was discovered now, they'd know she'd been hiding in order to listen. That would cause even more trouble. Her daring attempt at information gathering had better not backfire on her.

Henry's hearty voice replied. "No problem at all, Inspector. I'm expecting we'll be flooded with customers after lunch, as usual, but it's been fairly quiet here today, so far."

At that, Juliet's heart stopped. Those words might jog his memory and he might remember there had been a customer in here, that he hadn't seen leave.

Luckily, the inspector continued. "We're following up regarding the serious crime in Whistling Willow yesterday. Perhaps you heard of it? A retiree, who's a well-known local collector, was murdered."

"I have heard about it, of course. You know, I knew him on a professional basis, and a few people called me this morning to break the news. It's a crying shame that a helpless elderly gentleman can be murdered! What's the world coming to?"

Henry's voice was weighed down with sorrow. There was no hint of the scathing tone he'd used when discussing his rival with Juliet.

"We just need to check your whereabouts, at approximately two p.m. yesterday, sir. Just for the record, of course." Tennyson's tone was apologetic.

"Of course. I commend you for doing your job so thoroughly. I was here, of course, in my shop."

"You don't close up for lunch?" the inspector asked.

"Oh, no. Missing out on a potential customer? Not likely." Henry chuckled. But Juliet, from her vantage point, could see the sign that was on the back of the door's glass panel. Facing inward toward her, it read, "Back in Half an Hour."

If that sign was twisted around, then Henry could easily have closed up shop. He seemed to run this place on his own, and a man had to eat and use the bathroom. And, perhaps, drive one town over and kill a rival.

"There was also a missing book? I'm told you bid on it at the auction on Wednesday night?"

"Oh, that book." There was a smile in Henry's voice as he explained. "That book needn't concern you. I knew the market price for an antique like that would be beyond what I could resell. My clientele go more for furnishings and objects d'art, you know. So, I had no intention of acquiring it but knew that Mr. Douglas would want it at all costs. I regret to say I did something ungentlemanly," he confessed. "I drove up the bidding for a bit of drama, so that he'd end up paying more for it. I do like to support the auction house where I can."

He sniggered. To her astonishment, Tennyson sniggered, too.

He was going easy on him, and this was drastically unfair. Shouldn't he be testing this version instead of simply accepting it?

"Terrible thing for the family," Henry continued. "Had I foreseen this tragedy, I'd never have done such a thing. And please, pass on my condolences."

"I understand. It's good of you to have mentioned it," the inspector said. "I'll certainly pass on your condolences to the family. Both Mr. Douglas's daughter and brother are in town now."

"I hope they find peace," Henry said in a sanctimonious voice.

"Thanks for your time, and we'll be leaving now," the inspector said, as Juliet seethed.

"Glad you're doing such a thorough job. I have full confidence in the might of the law." Juliet rolled her eyes as Henry continued. "As I said, I've had a quiet morning. Just one customer, asking about old books." He paused. "That's strange. I didn't notice her leaving. I guess she must have done?" But he sounded unsure, as if he was looking around the shop now to see if he could spot her.

Freezing in place, not daring to breathe, Juliet made a panicked assessment of her escape routes. Things were not looking good. To get out now, she'd have to physically trample over the police.

If they realized who Henry was talking about, and discovered her in hiding, the inspector might end up bringing her in again for more questioning. He might even restrict her movement in the town or confine her to her guesthouse as a result of this suspicious behavior. Then she wouldn't be able to solve the case or even have a vacation at all.

“Sir!” Constable Coleridge’s voice split the air at exactly the same time Tennyson said, “Well, we’d better be off before we chase any other customers away.”

Juliet waited, twanging with tension. Coleridge had guessed who she might be, but Tennyson hadn’t been listening. He’d switched off and was heading for the door.

"But, sir!" With one last pleading bark, Coleridge rushed after his boss. The door swung shut, and they were gone.

“Strange,” Henry said, almost to himself. “I’m sure I didn’t see her leave. How odd. I could have made a sale there if I’d been quicker.”

Juliet didn’t dare to move a muscle. Henry was confused, but he wasn’t suspicious. And now that the police had gone, and he had an empty shop to himself, she fervently hoped that he might do something that would allow her to creep out unnoticed, so that he never knew she’d been listening out behind the wardrobe.

Luckily, her prediction was right. Henry, whistling softly to himself, walked to the other side of the counter, and she heard hinges squeak. That meant he must have gone into the office behind the counter, perhaps to make himself a nice cup of tea.

Holding her breath, she tiptoed out from behind the wardrobe, and crept back the way she had come, taking the same winding route through the antique furniture. And then she was out in the fresh, bright daylight, breathing a sigh of relief, and immediately checking the street for police cars.

There were none to be seen.

That had been harrowing. Heading back toward the bus stop, Juliet pondered over what she’d learned. She was sure that Henry had lied to the police. He hadn’t just been driving up the bidding. He’d desperately coveted that book.

The inspector had been soft on him, and the questions had been a simple formality, but Juliet had to admit that Henry hadn’t seemed rattled by them. He’d lied about his motives for bidding, but that was understandable in the circumstances. Nobody was going to say, in that situation, that they’d loathed the deceased and been furious to lose the auction.

What was most convincing to her was that when the police had left, he hadn’t breathed a sigh of relief, like she had when she’d finally been out of her risky situation. He'd thought he was alone and he was clearly a man who talked to himself. But he hadn't said, "Oh, my goodness, what a lucky escape, they've left at last." He'd simply shrugged it off, bemoaned the lack of a sale, and gone to make some tea, seeming relaxed and calm.

Juliet knew that human nature was full of surprises, but she didn't think that any man who'd killed in a fit of fury, would have the ability to remain so icy cool during and after a police interview, when he thought he was alone.

There would have been a muted 'Phew' at the very least. Or a 'Thank my lucky stars'. Or perhaps, an evil chuckle and a muttered 'I pulled the wool over their eyes!'

She was going to rule Henry out, for now, unless something happened to change her mind.

Thinking hard, she remembered who the other two bidders had been. One had been the elegantly dressed countess. She hadn't seemed like a serious buyer and had appeared to be bidding for the sake of it. She'd dropped out with a smile. The other man, however, had seemed much angrier. He'd been wearing a gray business suit, and he'd bid vigorously for that rare book until the price had soared out of his reach.

Had he been a local? She had no idea. He might be a local businessman, or else he might have arrived in town specifically for the auction. There was going to be only one way for her to find out, and that was by taking a look at the records.

Who had the organizer been? It had given the name on the signboard at the entrance. She'd taken note of it, but now the pressure was on, she couldn't actually remember it.

Juliet headed to the bus stop, thinking hard. As the bus pulled up and she climbed aboard, she tried to cast her mind back to that evening, remembering how full of excitement she'd been at attending this auction, and nervous, too, to be at an event all alone.

Alone. That word rang a bell.

Lone Oak Auctioneers. That was the name!

She quickly slid into her seat as the bus pulled away, rummaging in her soft, new, stylish leather purse for her phone. Perhaps she'd be lucky, and Lone Oak Auctioneers would be local. There was, after all, a large oak tree in the middle of the town square. Perhaps they'd named their business cleverly after the oak itself?

The results flashed up on her phone, and with a sense of triumph, Juliet saw her logic had taken her in the right direction. Lone Oak

Auctioneers was in Whistling Willow, and their offices were on the far side of the town square. That would mean she'd need to get off at the central bus stop. From there, it would be an easy walk.

It might even lead her past a bakery.

Or a salad shop, Juliet told herself firmly. A salad shop was what she needed now. There was only so much walking you could do to fend off the onslaught of carbs from a torrent of scones and pies.

The journey back to Whistling Willow passed quickly. Juliet divided her time between admiring the landscape – which you could see perfectly from a bus seat, as it allowed you to peek over the hedges that lined the back roads – and considering her approach when she headed into the auction house.

As she got closer to town, her nerves started surging again.

Wondering why she was feeling so frazzled, Juliet soon came up with the answer. It was because, with every confrontation she had, every question she asked, she must inevitably be getting closer to the killer.

"You can't stay invisible forever," she said, looking at the approaching town, and wondering if her next encounter would lead her to a murderer's hiding place.

CHAPTER SEVENTEEN

Juliet climbed off the bus at the middle stop, the one in the center of town, feeling optimistic about her new lead. It was late morning on a fine day, with clouds chasing each other across the sky to create cool, mottled sunshine. The center of town was bustling. Shops were busy, and Juliet could see tourists flooding in.

Heading straight to the auctioneer's office, Juliet was disappointed to see a "Back in Ten Minutes" sign on the door.

Whoever was looking after the shop for the day had taken a tea break, delaying her investigation.

However, on the bright side, this meant there was only one person in the office. It would hopefully be much easier to discreetly get some information from a single person, most likely a junior employee, than it would be to fight her way through a whole hierarchy of management.

In the meantime, Juliet used the opportunity to explore this side of the town square, which she hadn't gotten around to doing yet.

A store selling local craft gins was doing exceptionally well. Gins of all colors and flavors were lined up in the window. Sloe gin, apple gin, blue gin, botanical gin. Next door to it was an outdoor clothing store that drew her eye. The hiking boots displayed in the window looked so stylish and comfortable that she could imagine herself striding over the Cotswold hills.

And in the center of the town square, to her delight, was a small museum, which was dedicated to artifacts and treasures that had been discovered locally.

How amazing! She was sure that Oliver must spend a lot of time here, and she guessed that he must play a role in assessing all the finds. Didn't he say that there had recently been a rare coin discovered?

She knew she was supposed to be sleuthing. That was what she was here for. But since 'back in ten minutes' was putting a temporary pause on the sleuthing activities, and she was here on vacation, Juliet decided to seize the moment and head inside.

History, after all, was a fascinating topic. And right now, in the Cotswolds, she found that the history of the area was already intertwined, in her own mind, with the shy, charming smile and dark, appealing looks of Oliver Cambridge.

Thinking of Oliver, she walked in, paying the entrance fee to the attendant, and deciding she'd have a quick look around. She could come back another time, in better circumstances, for a longer visit.

As soon as she saw the interior, Juliet was entranced. This was a local gem. The museum was a converted house, with each of the rooms dedicated to a different angle of the area's history. The first room she peeked into had a notice outside, "Life in the Cotswolds."

The room was set up exactly as an old farmhouse might have been, a few centuries ago, with the furniture that real, ordinary people must have used. There was a narrow bed, with an embroidered coverlet, and a small, square dining room table with two chairs. An armchair nearby, with large, wooden arms, looked like it might have been comfortable – for a very tall person. Juliet wasn't sure about anyone else. Crockery and cutlery were set out on the table, a few basic, clay plates, and a delightfully colorful teapot in blue and white porcelain. A spinning wheel stood in the corner, cleverly arranged with yarn to look like it was in use, and the user had just stepped out for a moment.

Taken a ten-minute break, perhaps, she thought, chuckling to herself.

There was even a small bookcase, and drawn to it like a magnet, Juliet headed over, as close as she could get, respecting the "Please do not Touch" sign as she took in the details of the dusty, humble, weathered volumes. These were chosen deliberately to be old and shabby, she guessed, to give an accurate picture of what the poorer residents of the Cotswold area would have had access to.

The next room was dedicated to the historic finds in the area from the Roman times, with the Roman coins displayed in cases, each one complete with a map to show where it was found, and some historical facts on the coin itself. That was simply wonderful. Juliet felt enthralled. Imagine going out on a hike, and looking down, and spotting a dull, coppery-gold shape, that could result in a phenomenal find.

There were also pieces of pottery, amphoras – some whole, some fragments – as well as plates, knives, a weathered sandal, a horseshoe, and more. And then, her heart sped up as she saw an article written by none other than Oliver Cambridge. Carefully placed behind glass, the newspaper article was an explanation, by Oliver, on the different types of Roman pottery in the area, and how the use of different clays and techniques enabled the pieces to be accurately dated. It was delightfully well written – entertaining, funny and enlightening.

After reading it, Juliet resolved that her time in the museum was over for now. Although she wanted to go through every room and take in the fascinating details, she decided this was enough for today. She had an investigation to pursue. And more than that, she wanted to come back here with Oliver himself. After reading that short article, and hearing how he brought history alive, having him with her on a walk through the museum would be the biggest treat she could imagine.

Hoping that he'd agree to this outing – if she bought him dinner afterward, and feeling lighthearted at the thought, she hurried out and went back to the Lone Oak Auction House offices.

This time, the sign was removed and the door was open. Feeling hopeful, she headed into the darkly polished interior. Treading over deep brown, shiny parquet flooring, she headed to the magnificent dark wood desk, with carven legs and drawers, behind which the receptionist was sitting.

A woman of about forty, with short, shiny brown hair in a pixie cut, and a dark, tailored suit, blended in seamlessly with her elegantly furnished surroundings.

"Good morning," she said politely. "How can I help?"

"Good morning. I'm Juliet Page," she said. "I was at the auction the night before last, and I'm very interested to know more about who the bidders were. Is there a possibility of seeing a list?"

The woman raised a perfectly groomed eyebrow. "Why would you want to see this list?" she asked.

Juliet had to say something. She had to give a reason and was fumbling for a plausible lie. But even she was surprised by the words that came out of her mouth. They were the truth – in her hopes and dreams, at least.

"I want to become a dealer in rare, collectible books," she blurted out, as the woman's eyes widened.

Juliet was in shock. Had she really said that? Surely it was impossible for a humble librarian to have those aspirations? But now that she'd spoken the words, she'd confessed to a life goal that not even she had known about.

"Oh, I see." To her shock, the well groomed receptionist hadn't laughed, or told Juliet that this was impossible, or criticized her idea in any way at all. "Yes, then I suppose you want to get some connections."

Her accent was working in her favor now. She nodded, gulping as she realized that it hadn't been a plausible lie at all. Instead, it was an unattainable dream, but at least it was the truth.

"I'd really appreciate that," she said.

"You didn't bid at the auction yourself?" Maybe she was checking her credentials, Juliet thought.

"I'd only recently arrived in town. I didn't even know about it," she said.

The receptionist nodded. "It was arranged at quite short notice. The original date we chose conflicted with another event at the town hall, so we moved it forward by a week. You might not have heard that one of the main bidders unfortunately passed away yesterday? I believe there was an – an incident at his home." Her lips pressed together.

"Yes, I did hear about that, and it sounds so tragic," Juliet said.

"Now, let's see. Can I email you the list?"

She was going to be helpful. What a surprise. When she'd walked in, Juliet had expected this smart, reserved woman to be cold and unhelpful. But she didn't really want the list emailed without knowing who was who. If she could persuade this receptionist to discuss it on the spot, that would be the best scenario. Then, she'd benefit from her local knowledge.

"Do you have some time? Even just a few minutes?"

The receptionist was frowning now. Juliet could see she didn't have time.

"Even just one minute?" Juliet pleaded. "To quickly go through it with me, and explain who's who?"

"I suppose I can look over it with you, as long as it doesn't take too long," she relented.

She opened the folder and, after flipping through a few pages, removed a sheet of paper.

"The registered bidders are all well known. I guess you want the ones who bid on the books, seeing as how that's where your interest lies? Let me tell you who the successful bidders were, now." She ran a pearly-manicured finger down a list that was behind the open folder, so Juliet couldn't see.

"Yes, please."

"Countess Claymore. She loves her poetry books, but I see here she also bid successfully on two other books, so maybe she's extending her repertoire. Then there's Richard Banks. He also bid on a couple of books."

"Was he the man in the gray suit? A businessman?" Juliet asked, remembering how that man had angrily dropped out of the bidding after the price had soared.

"Yes, that's Mr. Banks."

There was something in the way she said his name that sparked Juliet's curiosity.

"Is there anything I should know about him?"

"No, no, not really at all," the receptionist said, now looking embarrassed.

"Are you sure?" Juliet was beginning to suspect there was something. It was the way the receptionist was suddenly avoiding her gaze.

"Well, I suppose if you're new in town, you wouldn't know," she said. "He's an estate agent who also used to run some auctions for us on a part-time basis, but Mr. Douglas – the person who passed away, in fact – unfortunately laid a complaint against him recently."

"He did?" Juliet was astonished to hear this.

"Yes. It wasn't well founded – he said that Mr. Banks had ignored a bid he'd made and awarded an item to the other bidder. Which was quite obviously untrue. I don't know why he would have done such a thing, but because of the complaint, Mr. Banks has not been able to run any auctions until it's been properly resolved."

"So he attended and bid instead?"

"Yes, he did. He's very supportive of our auctions," the receptionist said proudly.

"I guess, now that Mr. Douglas has passed away, the complaint would no longer be valid?" Juliet suggested.

"I suppose so," the receptionist said. "I didn't think about that, but you're right. With no complainant, it would automatically be dismissed."

Lights were flickering on in Juliet's mind as she thanked the receptionist. A whole Christmas tree full of them was now blazing.

She knew where to find Richard Banks. He was a real estate agent in town. And he had something she'd never expected to find – a double motive for wanting Alfred Douglas dead.

CHAPTER EIGHTEEN

"Banks Commercial and Residential," the discreet sign announced. Juliet walked up to it purposefully. This was where she was going to find answers, she was sure of it. In this well located office, which was upstairs from a small restaurant that was doing a busy lunch time trade.

The sound of laughter and the clink of cutlery, together with a whiff of garlic and braised meat, filled the air.

Heading up the stairs, lunchtime temptations were the last thing on Juliet's mind. She'd seen Richard Banks' face when he'd dropped out of the bidding. His demeanor had been furious. Anger had been visible in the set of his shoulders and the clench of his jaw. Now she understood the reason for it. Alfred had laid a complaint against him, one that had prevented him from holding auctions himself until it was resolved. Knowing Alfred's people skills, and remembering what his daughter had said about her attempted reconciliation with him, Juliet had a strong feeling that the complaint would not have been easily resolved.

So, furious and frustrated at every turn, Richard Banks had taken matters into his own hands.

Juliet was certain that he must be the killer.

And now, here he was. The upstairs office had a big glass window, and through it, she could see him shaking hands with a younger couple who looked excited and hopeful, as if they might be buying their first home. Seeing their faces gave Juliet a pang of nostalgia. She'd been in that same situation five years ago, a delighted newlywed looking forward to her married life. She hoped it worked out for this couple.

"There you go, then. Congratulations." Uttering the words in a booming voice, Mr. Banks steered the couple to the door, and Juliet stood aside as they passed. Then, he invited her in with a sweep of his arm.

Now that she was face to face with him, she was aware what a big man he was in every respect. Broad-shouldered, tall, with large, fleshy hands and a voice that would have done justice to an opera singer. Today, he was all smiles, and there was no trace of the frowning anger that had hung over him at the auction. He was wearing a black pinstripe suit and a magenta tie.

"Come in, come in. I am Richard Banks, your local real estate specialist." The small office was equipped with two desks – one grander, by the window, and one smaller, where Juliet guessed an assistant worked. From the open file on the assistant's desk, she guessed he or she must be out to lunch.

Mr. Banks ushered her over to the larger of the two desks and pulled out a visitor's chair, upholstered in comfortable blue plaid.

"Do I know you?" he asked, fixing her with a keen gaze as she sat down.

"I've just arrived in town," she said. "My name's Juliet Page."

But now, worry was uncoiling inside her. Did Mr. Banks remember her from the auction? She'd thought his attention would have been fixated on the bidding debacle. But even during a debacle, people could still be observant and remember what they'd seen.

She would need to be careful, because if he knew she'd been at the auction, he'd start to wonder why she was asking questions she should already know. He would grow suspicious, and then, she wouldn't get the information she needed.

Dealing with a violent and unpredictable killer, things might even get worse. Twisting her fingers together, Juliet made a mental note of which way the door had opened in case she needed to get through it fast.

"So, Ms. Page. How can I help you today?" he asked, heading over to the leather director's chair. It creaked as he sat down opposite her.

Juliet's mind was racing. She needed a plausible story, a reason for confronting Mr. Banks. She couldn't just blurt out the question of whether he was a killer. And nor could she suddenly inquire about his whereabouts at two p.m. yesterday. He'd be suspicious. And from the intelligent gleam in his gray eyes, she knew that if he became suspicious, he'd figure her out in a flash.

Nothing for it but to continue with the story that wasn't quite true, but definitely wasn't a lie.

"I'm just putting out feelers," she said, her mouth suddenly dry, "but I was wondering if there might be a small retail space available for rent anywhere in town?"

"In this town? Whistling Willow?" he asked.

"Yes," Juliet said. Her stomach was twisting now, not only from nerves at having to question a suspected killer, but now also with a weird sense of excitement at voicing her dream aloud. “Yes, I’ve not made any decisions yet, but I was wondering about price and location. That kind of thing?”

"So this would obviously be a rental? You're going to start your own little store? Excellent idea!" There was such confidence in his voice that, for a heady moment, it seemed impossible that her plans *couldn’t* succeed. “What’s your line of work?” he asked.

“Books,” she said.

“Ah, books!” He chuckled. “I think it’s time there was some healthy competition in town for our local bookstore owner.”

“No,” Juliet said, banishing the thought of Elizabeth’s haughty face and snobbish attitude, and steering the conversation to where she needed it to go. “Not new books. I’m a lover of old books. Collector’s items, historic works, antiques.”

“Ah. Even better.” But now he was looking at her closely, and she felt a thrill of concern that he was seeing her in a different light. “There’s definitely a space for that in this town, with so many tourists interested in the culture and history of the Cotswolds. What sort of size?”

She hadn’t thought about size.

Smilingly, she shrugged. "Well, since I have no idea what the rental price is, I'm not looking at any particular size. I'd just like to know what's available and if I can make it work."

She felt a sense of deep regret. If only this pipe dream could come true, but she didn't have a budget for more than the occasional charity shop purchase. In reality, she was nothing but a time waster.

However, she reminded herself that everyone was a time waster until the sale was made, and that if Richard Banks was a killer, he deserved to be in prison, and not selling up a storm in this plush upstairs office.

“Let’s have a look.” Banks pulled out a laminated map of the town, uncapped a blue whiteboard marker, and, with unerring precision, began circling sites. Juliet waited, feeling the odd sensation as if she was living two different lives.

One life, a librarian on a budget, trying to clear her name.

And another life, a woman following her dreams and plunging headlong into a new life.

The sensation was so weird that it sent goosebumps up and down her spine.

"This one is about a hundred yards from the tearoom. Very good site. It's small, a real hole in the wall size, which is why it's standing vacant. It's between a leatherware store and a general gift shop, so very well located. I'll be able to negotiate a special deal for your rental, because of the shop's small size. Fine for books, obviously, as they don't take up too much space. There's also an apartment above it, which could be included in the deal. Live and work locally – what shorter walk to work than going downstairs?" he asked.

He named the rental, and she felt her stomach churn. Was it affordable in her dream scenario? Could the other Juliet, living a parallel life, make it work financially? She didn't know, of course. There was far too much else to consider. She wasn't even entirely sure what the exchange rate was, and would have to convert this into dollars for a better picture.

In any case, what was she doing? She was here to catch a killer!

As the whiteboard marker squeaked again, circling another sought-after site, Juliet realized she'd been thoroughly sidetracked by her own imagination.

Taking a deep breath, she waited for Banks to finish telling her all about the benefits of this site.

Then, pulling herself together, she asked, "Tell me, rare books. Is there much of an interest for them in town? Someone mentioned you were an auctioneer?"

Banks blinked as if surprised by the sudden turn the conversation had taken.

"You're right. I am an auctioneer," he said, then hesitated. He was about to speak, but then stopped himself. Suddenly, the charismatic confidence he'd been exuding disappeared.

"Well, until recently I was an auctioneer," he muttered. "There was a stumbling block in the road, but it's been removed now."

"What do you mean by that?" she asked.

"Nothing," he said. "Nothing. Just referring to a recent episode that I was personally involved in."

"What episode was it?" she asked, wanting to push forward and get the information.

But his face was different now. His eyes were narrowed. This man was clearly recalling the past, in vivid detail. What exactly was he remembering? If only she could read his mind. Was he just thinking back to the humiliation of having to drop out of the bidding, bested by a man who'd lodged a professional complaint against him?

Or was he remembering something more violent? Like the moment he attacked that man with a blunt object?

The problem was that thinking back to the auction must have jogged his memory. He looked at Juliet again, this time with a different expression.

"I have a very good memory for faces, and I'm certain I've seen you before," he said. Then he snapped his fingers loudly, causing Juliet to jump. "Were you at the auction yourself? I'm sure I remember you sitting next to – what's his name, that historical expert I sold the cottage to – Oliver Cambridge? Were you with Oliver?"

Now, the situation had done a turnaround, and she was unpleasantly in the spotlight herself. No way could she deny it. He wouldn't believe her, and she couldn't tell such a bare-faced lie.

"Yes, I was," she admitted.

His wide brow furrowed in a frown, and suddenly, his face didn't look nearly as genial as it had done when she'd first walked in.

"But why didn't you say so?" he asked. "Why did you come in and say you were a potential customer? Are you even interested in a retail space? I'm beginning to think otherwise."

This had all turned so wrong. She'd thought her story was plausible and that it would work, but she'd reckoned without this man's talent for recognizing faces.

But was he the killer?

"Why are you here?" Banks pressured her, his gaze intense.

It was time to make a snap decision on how much of the truth to tell. What was her gut advising her?

Her gut was advising her that she should turn and run, and that the door opened outwards, and that there was every chance this man was the killer.

What she did now could be pivotal in proving her own innocence fast. If she was brave enough to ride this situation out, and dug deep for a confidence she wasn't sure she possessed, then she might get valuable information, even now.

All she had to figure out, in one nanosecond, was what she should say.

CHAPTER NINETEEN

With her heart banging in her chest, summoning up all the confidence she could muster, Juliet replied.

"Mr. Banks, I was at the auction because I have an interest in rare books. Alfred Douglas learned about that, and invited me to his house, to teach me about fakes and replicas. I found him dead! He must have been murdered shortly before I arrived! And the valuable Oliver Twist was missing!"

Now, it was her turn to watch his face as she dropped the bombshells.

His eyes and mouth both widened, and he blinked rapidly.

"You found his body?" he asked.

"I did! So you'll understand why I am looking for closure. I know things were difficult between the two of you."

Now was the challenging part. He'd know that she suspected him of being the killer. This was where Mr. Banks might get angry – and she might have to make that dash for the door.

But to her astonishment, he got entirely the wrong end of the stick.

"Yes," he said. "You've come to the right place if you are looking for a frank opinion on Alfred and those forgeries. I understand why you – well, why you made an excuse for seeing me. Not really easy to broach a sensitive subject like that up front."

It was hard not to look just as shocked as Mr. Banks had done.

He thought she was here to ask about forgeries? If he was the killer, that would be the last thing on his mind. But while he was talking more openly, maybe she could check his alibi, if she was clever about it?

"I guess it's one of those shocking events where you'll always remember where you were at the time," she said, quirking an eyebrow at him.

"Well, at the time, I was showing that lovely couple who left as you arrived, around their dream home a mile out of town," he said. "It's chilling to think that while I was convincing them that the second bedroom was big enough for their needs, and awakening them to the potential of the large garden, my long-time rival was being murdered."

Aha. The opportunity to boast about a recent property sale had neatly confirmed his whereabouts at the time of the crime. She relaxed just a little, allowing herself to settle into the well upholstered seat. Now she knew he wasn't the killer, this could all take place in a less pressurized mindset.

"Actually, I was very interested in that rental space as well," she said, deciding to keep this side of the relationship open, now that the idea was lodged in her head. "It is a dream of mine to have a rare bookstore one day. Maybe not right now, but one day."

"I'm glad to hear that," he said. "One should always follow one's dreams." But he looked at her with an inquiring expression as if he knew there was more to be discussed.

"I would like to know more about the forgeries," she said.

She hadn't known they had caused such a stir. But this rival of Alfred's had clearly known. Perhaps he'd followed the story.

"Well," he said, "It's a long, complicated story, and it ended with Alfred complaining that I had missed a bid while running an auction. He actually laid a formal complaint against me."

"Really?" Juliet didn't want to give away that she had already known that.

"But it started with me laying a complaint against him for having sold me an old book that was a forgery."

Now, her eyes flew wider. She didn't know where this was heading but it must be important.

"When did this happen?"

"About six months ago. I missed out on an auction where he bid for a few books. I wanted one of them for a client – a first edition of a Jane Austen, so I asked him if he'd sell. Surprisingly, after some quibbling over price, and of course, throwing a few insults my way, he agreed. Said he'd post it up. When it arrived, it was an obvious fake!"

"It was?" Juliet felt shocked.

"I contacted him immediately. He blew up, called me a fraud, refused to believe me at all for a while." Banks sighed heavily as he remembered the conflict. "I eventually drove to his house and showed him the book. He accepted that I was correct, after another long argument, and refunded me my money. Although he didn't say so, I got the impression it was a recurring problem, and that this wasn't the first time it had happened. You know, I'm very perceptive at reading between the lines."

“Do you believe that he sold it, knowing it was a fake?” Juliet said, feeling fascinated by what she’d learned.

"I don't think he knew. You may have seen how he stores all his books. He's extremely protective about their condition. Each one is shipped in a plastic packet, protected from the elements? The problem is that with the plastic on, you can’t see what the book looks like inside, and he might not have checked. I think he didn’t check it, but took it from the shelf and wrapped it and posted it to me as soon as he’d received my check in the mail.”

“So that means someone was stealing his books? And replacing them with forgeries?”

"That's exactly what I think," the estate agent told her, folding his arms decisively. "I think he had a serious problem. It was an insider job, it must have been. Someone who visited him regularly must have been picking and choosing what they wanted and getting forgeries made to replace them. That was what I told him."

“And did he do anything about it? Did he call the police?” Juliet asked.

Banks shrugged. “Knowing Alfred, he was too egotistical to get the police involved. Calling them would mean admitting that he’d been swindled. That wouldn’t have sat well with him, as you can imagine.”

“I only met him for a short time, but yes, I can imagine that,” Juliet admitted.

“I don’t think he ever got to the bottom of it.” Thoughtfully, Banks tapped the desk. “Although, maybe he did,” he added. “Maybe he did discover who was doing it, and when the thief realized he knew, they killed him.”

***

While she’d been speaking to Mr. Banks, her mind whirling with the information he’d given her, Juliet had heard her phone buzzing in her purse. Luckily, she’d put it on silent for the interview. As soon as she was out of the small upstairs office, she quickly pulled it out and turned the ringtone back on. Who had been messaging her so insistently?

It could be Inspector Tennyson wanting to speak to her again. If so, she'd need to call him back urgently.

But it wasn’t the inspector. Instead, she had several messages, all from Mike.

The first one said, *"But Juliet! We need to try again!"*

Then, the next one: *"Why aren't you replying to my messages? Please let me know if we can try again. It was a mistake! I promise! You've always been the one!"*

The third one read, *"I've just heard from your lawyer. Is this some kind of a joke?"*

The fourth one: "*I guess it's not a joke. I guess you're actually being serious about this. I am a broken man. You have emotionally wrecked me!"*

Then the fifth and final one. *"Alright! If that's what you want then I'm going to put our apartment up for sale and move in with Jess!"*

Standing at the bottom of the stairs, with the mouthwatering smells from the restaurant drifting out, Juliet read these messages, with a sense of unreality.

It seemed as if Mike had been through a rapid metamorphosis of their relationship. These texts represented an arc so steep that Juliet was struggling to follow it.

She read them all again, looking at the timestamps, her eyes boggling out of her head.

Surprisingly, after the rollercoaster ride that the past couple of days had been, she didn't feel devastated, or traumatized, or even just sad. Her main emotion now was one of relief. Mike had shown his true colors, and she was well out. She might have left him a few years too late, but at least she'd left him.

"It was a learning curve," Juliet muttered to herself as she walked away from the real estate offices, below that tasty smelling restaurant. "It was five years I invested in learning about human nature, retrospectively."

Not just retrospectively, she mused, as she headed for the main street. Her lessons had all been there along the way, ready for her to study them. It was just that she'd been embedded in denial, and in a comfort zone. Now she was all the way out of that mindset. Strangely, it made her feel more equipped for the scary and unfamiliar task she was doing now.

And thanks to what Richard Banks had told her, she knew where to start.

It was the books. This entire murder had to be related to the books. And more importantly, to the fake books. The ones that had mysteriously appeared in Alfred Douglas's collection.

Those fake books were significant, Juliet felt sure of it.

Somebody close to Alfred must have been stealing them. Somebody very close to him. Perhaps, someone that he had trusted. He hadn't known about this, but somebody in that incredibly neat and clean house had arrived, betrayed him, stolen a number of books which presumably they had sold, and then decided that the best solution was murder.

The problem was that this crotchety, egotistical man hadn't had many friends, and Juliet didn't know how she could keep track of his visitors.

She wondered suddenly if the answers lay in the books themselves.

Was there a way of finding out which books had been replaced by fakes? Would Alfred himself, angry and with a bruised ego, have kept track of such a thing?

He hadn't had many people close to him, for obvious reasons. So perhaps he'd kept a diary or a journal to share his life's ups and downs with – well, himself.

Would the police have looked in such a book if they'd even found it? They'd had ample opportunity to search his house and take whatever evidence they had needed.

Therefore, anything that was still in the house would have been ignored by the police.

"Wait a minute!" Juliet said the words aloud. Stopping in the middle of the cobbled street, she heard a tourist behind her say, "Oops! Excuzez moi!" as they swerved past.

She was too stunned by the reality of what she was prepared to do to be able to move a muscle.

How exactly had she gone from being a law abiding librarian, to becoming somebody who was willing to clandestinely search a house to find a clue to clear herself and incriminate a killer?

She was remembering the journal that Alfred had carried with him at the auction and had written in. That journal must be somewhere. Alfred had clearly used it a lot, and if the police had found it, then surely even Inspector Tennyson would have gotten some leads?

As she strode along, Juliet began wildly justifying her actions in advance.

It would depend on a lot of factors. Firstly, if the house was unlocked. She was not prepared to break into a home – and it would be insane to even think of it, because Inspector Tennyson would find out, and she'd be locked in the local prison before you could say "Yes, sir!"

Fascinating as Whistling Willow was, and keen as she was to explore all its nooks and crannies, Juliet did not want to get a closer look at the inside of the town's holding cell. The interview room where she'd been questioned was as far as she wanted to go in that direction.

Logically, though, somebody should be there. Alfred had a brother, Basil. Surely he would have come to pack up the house? Surely somebody would be there after a death in the family? With such a large, tidy house, Alfred must employ servants, even though she'd seen no sign of any maid. The house was squeaky clean.

It would depend on fate, she decided, turning onto the road that would lead her back to Alfred Douglas's house. Fate would decide if she got beyond the front door.

Striding up the hill, Juliet fervently hoped that fate would be on her side.

CHAPTER TWENTY

She didn't know where she would find the clues she needed, but Juliet was becoming more and more convinced that she needed to look for them. If Alfred had had several rare books stolen, he must have been livid. He would have been hunting for the thief.

And maybe he had found the thief, but the thief had acted first.

She'd never wanted to set foot again inside the room where she'd seen such a terrible sight, but she was going to have to do just that. Assuming she even got that far.

"You are not wriggling in through a window," Juliet warned herself as she raised the brass knocker. "Not under any circumstances."

The house looked quiet and neat. If there had been fingerprint dust all over the knocker and the doorknob, it had been cleaned away. It all looked as new and shiny as it had done the last time she'd been here.

She brought the knocker down and waited, twisting her fingers together, hoping that she'd be able to find something she needed, in the place where she guessed it would be.

Footsteps approached. Not heavy footsteps, but light, quick ones. A moment later, the door was opened.

Juliet found herself staring at the woman whose presence had been hinted at, through the extreme cleanliness of the house, but who she'd never set eyes on until now.

Dressed in a dark gray outfit, with black slip-on shoes and a black cap on her head, the housekeeper looked haunted. Her face was pale and Juliet saw lines of tension there that made it hard to guess her age. Thirty-five, perhaps, although she looked a decade older?

"Good afternoon," she said in a reserved tone that vibrated with stress.

"Good afternoon," Juliet replied politely. She'd got as far as the door being opened. Now, how to capitalize on this important lead? Inside the dark, cool entrance hall, she saw a few arrangements of flowers were set on the table.

"I've come to pay my respects," she said. "I'm Juliet Page, and I was introduced to Mr. Douglas at a book event."

The housekeeper nodded. “You’ll be wanting his brother, Basil, I imagine?”

“Um, yes,” Juliet said.

“His daughter is no longer in town,” the housekeeper continued, hollowly.

That would be the daughter who told Juliet how badly her father had treated everyone, including underpaying the staff. Juliet guessed that even though the housekeeper had been treated so badly, she must still be upset by the death to look like this.

“Yes, Basil,” she said, already trying to figure out how she could distract Basil for long enough to take a look around.

But it seemed that luck was on her side – or, as her mother always used to say when embarking on something scary with the hope of good results, “Fortune favors the brave.” Because the housekeeper replied, “Basil is still in town, and will be back in about ten minutes.”

“I’ll wait,” Juliet said, her heart speeding up.

The housekeeper headed to the first door on the left, leading into the perfectly furnished living room that Juliet had seen last time. She ushered her in and asked if she wanted any refreshments.

“No, thank you,” Juliet replied, sitting down and trying to appear at ease.

With a wordless nod, the housekeeper left. As soon as she had walked out of the doorway, Juliet jumped to her feet and tiptoed to the door.

Peering out, she saw that the housekeeper was trudging to the end of the corridor. As Juliet watched, she headed up the stairs.

She was going up to the bedrooms, and that gave Juliet the chance she needed.

Walking on silent feet over the shiny floorboards, holding her breath as she tiptoed along, Juliet headed all the way down the corridor to the library. This was more than just a library, she was sure. It had been Alfred’s haven, the place he’d felt most comfortable. The writing desk and the armchair both convinced her that he’d used this room as a study, as well as a reading retreat.

The fresh, cool air filtered through the door as she pushed it open. Cool, dry, climate controlled. The perfect environment for storing valuable books.

Would the police have searched the desk already? The only thing on it was a leather blotter and a dark red mug containing some stationery items. Then again, casting her memory back, she couldn’t remember it being different last time. Maybe there hadn't been anything on the desk then, either.

The desk drawers opened smoothly. In the first one was more stationery – a few pens, an empty notebook, some pencils and a sharpener. In the second drawer, she saw brown papers, string, and a few lengths of bubble wrap. If Alfred had posted books out, he must have kept the materials here.

There was no diary, though. No personal journal.

Surely there must be one? Where would he have kept it?

The armchair was still in place, although she only dared to look at it from out of the corner of her eye.

The memory of Alfred slumped in it was still too vivid. The armchair faced the shelves of his collection. A collection that had been tampered with. Had he written in his journal while sitting in that chair?

She headed over to the shelves, looking at each of the books, admiring their flawless spines, the quality of the paper, the gleam of the gold lettering on some of the more expensive volumes. Her gaze picked up so many familiar names, so many noble volumes that resonated with history. And their condition! These were all on the grade of Fine to Very Good.

Again, the irony struck her that the best old books were obtained from the shelves of non-readers, who hadn't subjected them to wear and tear.

He wouldn't have left a notebook there, because a thief had been going through this prized collection. Knowing time was running out and feeling more and more uneasy that she wasn't where she was supposed to be, Juliet headed to the side of the library where the more ordinary books were shelved.

No thief would have bothered with these. They were your average secondhand, tatty paperbacks. Maybe some of them had come as bulk deals with more valuable books, and he'd kept them 'just because'. Because that was what book people did. An empty shelf was unthinkable.

He was a knowledgeable collector, and wouldn't have wanted to disturb his fine, rare books by pulling a journal in and out of the stack. But these books? Well, they were already well thumbed, and in tatters, and only worth a dollar or two, to a reader who would pull and bend and damage and love them all over again.

With fresh eyes and resolve, Juliet scanned the bookshelf, looking for what she now strongly suspected was there.

A slim journal, hard cover, black in color. It would be like a stripe of negative space between all these scuffed, faded spines.

Looking and looking along the rows of books, Juliet felt a sinking of her heart. It wasn't here. Her theory had been good, but it hadn't worked out. This valuable book was nowhere in sight.

And even as she had the thought, she saw it.

There it was. A slim, black spine. Looking exactly like negative space. Her hands trembled as she reached out and pulled out of the row.

It was far too risky to read it in here.

She was going to have to take it to the living room.

Clutching the journal in her hand and feeling uncomfortably like a thief, even though she hadn't removed it from the house, Juliet crept out of the office and hurried back along the corridor, veering into the living room and perching on the edge of a velvet-covered, antique chair.

Hands unsteady with nerves, she opened the journal.

The first thing she realized, frowning incredulously, was that Alfred's handwriting was terrible. Really terrible! So bad that he could have been a doctor. The scribbles on every page seemed influenced by his mood and emotion. Anger produced jagged peaks of handwriting, with blue ink welling out of the pen – it was clear that he had used a fountain pen. Nothing else would be acceptable, of course.

"What does this say?" she muttered, holding the page further away, and then closer up. Neither angle helped.

She was going to have to get into tune with this man's handwriting in order to figure it out.

Turning the page, she looked at one scrawled paragraph, and then a few of the scribbled words opposite. Nothing made sense. She focused harder.

Then she managed to figure out one word. That must be 'devious'.

Devious. So if that large sack shaped letter was a capital D, then maybe that one was Delinquent. And that was a B Boring show. Badly written novel. Boundless incompetence. Word after word made sense as she read through his daily jottings, feeling as if she'd learned a new language at speed.

She paged through the book, her senses sharp and alert.

There was a word she needed. Thief. It jumped out at her, and she homed in on it,

"A thief has been stealing my books."

Below this were closely jotted observations, written in a smaller hand. As if he had been thoughtfully pondering while he read the words.

"On days when I am out. Monday 29th, Thursday 3rd, Day after Summer Bank Holiday!"

"Using my packaging!"

"Posting the books somewhere? Must be!"

"Replacement: cheap forgeries!" That sentence was so angry that the dot under the exclamation mark had made an actual hole in the paper.

"Set a trap for them? Track the parcels? Ask Basil to assist?"

And then, below that, in triumphant capital letter, *"I KNOW WHO IT IS!"*

Juliet caught her breath. He knew! He'd figured it out. She still had no idea, though.

Or maybe she did.

"Maybe I do," she whispered, as light dawned. Maybe she knew, too. Because there was only one logical answer, and she was going to have to move fast to prove it. There was no time to put the book back where she'd found it. Instead, she shoved it under the cushion of the chair she'd been sitting on.

She knew what the next step was, and where she needed to go, to prove the theory that would lead her to the killer.

CHAPTER TWENTY ONE

Fizzing with excitement, Juliet headed for the front door. But, as she reached it, it rattled loudly. She stopped, breathing hard, planting her feet on the entrance hall's carpet as the door swung open.

Basil Douglas had arrived home.

He was a tall man with a slightly stooped posture, who looked a few years younger than Alfred, but with the same sharp features and haughty air. His eyebrows were well groomed, he wore an expensive looking tweed jacket, and his brown hair was mostly covered by a gray deerstalker hat.

For a moment, Juliet wondered if she should tell him the theory that had just come to her in the form of a brainwave.

Better not to, she decided. Because what if he inadvertently warned the guilty person?

Instead, she smiled charmingly.

"Good afternoon, Mr. Douglas. I'm so very sorry about your brother's death. I met him when I arrived here on vacation, and I came here to offer my condolences."

Basil raised his eyebrows. "You have? Well, thank you."

He spoke in a brusque manner. She didn't know if that was because he was numb with grief, or because he was a brusque person. Remembering what Geraldine had said about her uncle, she suspected it was the latter.

At least Basil Douglas didn't know who she was. For the time being, anyway, and by sight. It would be better not to give him her name, because he might recognize it.

"I arrived a little early and I've got an appointment in town, so I have to rush off, but I'm glad to meet you in person. And, once again, my condolences."

He raised an eyebrow. "There's no need to overstate things, you know. I'm beginning to wonder if all you townsfolk expect me to make some kind of a donation in my brother's name?" His mouth twisted cynically. "Repair the town hall roof, or something of the kind? I'm afraid that won't happen."

Juliet's eyes flew wide. What a rude man!

At least his rudeness meant he hadn't bothered to ask her name. And after a reply like that, a quick getaway was justified.

"Thank you," she said again. She had no idea why. It just seemed the polite thing to say.

He turned away from her. "Miss Edmund?" he called in a sharp voice. "I'm back. I hope you haven't gone off duty yet! Bring me some tea, and get these flowers off the hall table. They're cluttering things up."

While his attention was focused on his environment, Juliet slipped through the still-open door, and hurried down the garden path, passing the large, tan Land Rover parked half in the road, that clearly belonged to Basil Douglas.

Then, she hustled back to town.

***

Next stop, the place where she hoped her theory would be proven right – or wrong, Juliet thought, as she hurried down the winding road that led to the town square. The afternoon was clouding over dramatically. The sun was blanketed by dark, threatening clouds – each one with a silver lining, though, she noticed optimistically.

She hurried along the cobbled street to the post office.

There was an old fashioned red letter box outside, not just a decorative feature, because the collection times were displayed on it. The post office's cheerful signage, the oval red with the white wording, was displayed on the shop front.

Hoping it would be possible to get this information, she walked inside.

There was a short queue at the counter, with a few people waiting patiently in line to send parcels. Juliet saw that there seemed to be an automated parcel system in place. But almost nobody could use it. Everyone was struggling with the sensor, and the label printer, and the weighing system, and so the kindly looking woman, in a blue jacket, with her strawberry blond hair tied back in a neat French braid, was permanently stationed there.

She was basically doing the work of the automated system, while offering a stream of cheerful chatter at the same time.

"Yes, that's right, luv. You put it just like that and now, wait until you hear it go beep. Okay, let me do it for you. There you go. Beep!

Now we stick the label on just like that, and now you just put your card in the machine there, and it'll charge it for you."

"Oh, thank you so much," the grateful woman, who Juliet thought sounded Australian, replied.

"Yes, our automated system is really wonderful, innit? Technology is a great thing. I've worked here for ten years, and it's wonderful to see the improvements," the post office helper said, without a trace of irony in the words. "Next, please!"

Juliet decided that in order to engage in conversation with this lovely woman, she needed to have something to post. The choice was fairly simple. There were a few postcards, some items of stationery, and a couple of curios. One of the curios was a tin box with 'A Present From Whistling Willow', and a picture of a terrier with a red bow on his collar.

That would be perfect. Grabbing the tin box, Juliet got into line.

The line shuffled forward. It was going slowly, but her thoughts were surging ahead at high speed. By the time she reached the front, she had a good idea about how to broach the topic.

"Oh, goodness!" she said, looking at the machine and recoiling as if it was a scary killer robot. "How do I work this?"

"Let me help!" The friendly assistant rushed forward. "It's all very simple once you get the hang of it. Do you have a packet for that? You'll need a packet. Where's it going to?"

"To San Francisco," she replied. "I'm posting it to my sister."

"Oh, how lovely. She's a dog lover is she? This is one of our best selling items. They also come with cats, but those have sold out."

"Yes, she is a dog lover."

Checking there was nobody in the line behind her, Juliet tried to nudge the conversation in the right direction.

"I've been in town a couple of days," she said, as the woman patiently typed Sarah's address into the machine, reading it from Juliet's phone. "And I couldn't help hearing about this terrible murder."

"Oooh, it's shocking. Shocking! We're all so rattled by it, I can tell you. My mum, who lives down in Bath, is calling me twice daily now to check I'm safe," the woman said.

"And what do you say to her?" Juliet asked curiously.

"I tell her every time, I'm safe so far. It's my belief that Mr. Douglas was killed by an enemy. He was – well, he was rather aggressive at times, you know? Probably due to personal stress, I'm sure," she said forgivingly. "But there weren't many people in town who didn't get the rough side of his tongue."

She pressed a button, and the label rolled smoothly out of the printer. Juliet stuck it on the front of the envelope, making sure it was nice and straight.

"Did you ever get the rough side of his tongue?" she asked, putting her credit card in the slot as directed.

"Us, here? Oh, no, he knew better than to be rude to me. He was always polite when he came in here because I lay down the law. There's to be no rudeness when we are dealing with the Royal Mail! Only polite efficiency," she beamed.

"Did he post out a lot of books?" Juliet asked.

"Not that many. I don't think he liked getting rid of his books. They were very dear to him."

Now for the important question.

"Did anyone else ever post his books for him? I heard gossip in town that he sometimes used to send someone else. Most recently, the day after the Summer Bank Holiday."

"I was working that day." The woman frowned as she headed over to the parcel container and placed the parcel inside. "Now you've got me thinking."

She leaned over and tapped a few keys on the computer screen.

"Yes. He actually did post something to Doncaster, but he didn't bring it in himself." Light dawned. "He sent his housekeeper, Ellie Edmund. She's not the most cheerful person in the world, either. But then, nor would I be if I worked for him." Lowering her voice, she offered this tidbit of information in a near whisper.

Juliet's heart was pounding. She couldn't believe that, at last, she had the answer. It was obvious! It had been all along. The puzzle pieces were falling into place at last. But would she be believed? That was the question.

Thanking the attendant politely, she left, heading straight across the square to where the police station was located.

She hoped that Inspector Tennyson would believe her – and that he'd agree to make a swift arrest. Everything hinged on what would happen in the next few minutes.

CHAPTER TWENTY TWO

Juliet hoped that this was the second, and last, time she'd be walking into the police station. This time, not as a suspect, but with information that would provide the breakthrough in the case. This could lead to the killer's arrest. She knew she was right – but would the police accept her version?

Adrenaline surged in her veins, and a crash of thunder from behind her made her jump. The weather was reflecting her mindset, with an unseasonal late summer thunderstorm brewing.

She headed straight up to the counter, where the officer on duty gave her a sharp look. He clearly recognized her as a person of interest in the murder investigation that had shaken the town.

"I'd like to speak to Inspector Tennyson," Juliet said calmly.

He eyed her for a few more seconds, as if wondering whether she was about to turn herself in.

"The inspector isn't here," he said. "He's out, following an important lead."

"But I have an important lead!" Juliet said. "I need him to come back here so that I can give it to him!"

"Do you want to wait in the interview room?" The officer raised an eyebrow.

"No! I don't want to wait in the interview room!" She had the distinct sense that this man hadn't given up on the idea she was somehow involved in the crime. "I need you to please call him on his phone."

"Alright." Reluctantly, as if he was very disappointed that she hadn't walked in to confess to the crime, he picked up the phone and dialed. He waited. Then, he uttered a few terse words, and hung up.

"I'm afraid that the inspector has his phone turned off. Or else, he doesn't have signal. I've left a message."

"Do you know where he is? This is urgent."

"I certainly don't know. When our detectives head off on an urgent mission, they don't broadcast their whereabouts," the officer replied. "I've left a message. And that's the most I can do."

Her heart was racing as she remembered Basil's words to the housekeeper, words that she'd clearly heard just before she left.

"I hope you haven't gone off duty yet."

That meant the housekeeper was going off duty. Juliet was sure she'd only stayed on at work another couple of days after the murder so that she would avoid any suspicion. But now, with the valuable Charles Dickens first edition tucked away in her bag, and the brother ready to pack up the house, Juliet had a strong hunch that she was going to go off duty – and never come back. Why would she? She'd gotten away with murder, free and clear.

"Please, tell him to call me as soon as he can," she implored the stony-faced officer. "He knows my number. I'll keep my phone open."

She turned and walked out, relieved to be back in the buzz of the town square. As the dark clouds loomed, people were dismantling their sidewalk displays, and tourists were opening umbrellas of all shades and sizes as they rushed to complete their shopping before the storm broke.

"I need to go back," Juliet said. "I have to retrieve that journal. Ellie Edmund might notice it, or be hunting for it, and take it with her."

That journal documented Alfred's suspicions. Without it, the housekeeper could simply claim that she'd been told to post the books. And Juliet was very sure that the books would have been sent to a name and address that didn't directly link to the buyer of the stolen books. There would have been a cut-out involved. Of course, there would, with everything now digitally recorded.

There was no time to wait! The killer might be doing a runner, and the evidence might be going along with her. Juliet had to get there first, grab the evidence, and corral the suspected killer.

In that case, she needed help.

And it wouldn't be a bad thing to have a witness, either.

With a sense of hope and expectancy, she got out her phone. Standing under the overhang next to the police station, she dialed Oliver's number.

He answered on the second ring.

"Hello! Oliver speaking!" He sounded cheery and upbeat, as charming on the phone as he was in real life.

"Oliver, it's Juliet," she said.

"Juliet! I'm so glad you called. I've just wrapped up a site evaluation, and I'm driving back into town. I was going to ask you if you wanted to go for a coffee or a glass of wine. I've been thinking about you," he added.

She had to admit it, her heart sped up in a way that had nothing to do with the pressure of the situation.

"I've been thinking about you," she said, the words making her heart feel warm, before the intensity of her predicament rushed back. "But before we have that glass of wine, I was wondering if you could help me with something. It's to do with the murder, and it's urgent. I believe I've found the killer!"

There was an astonished silence.

"You've found the killer? Where are you?" Oliver asked.

"I'm standing right outside the police station," she said. "But I need to go up to Alfred Douglas's house. Will you come with me?"

"I'll be there in – in exactly three minutes," Oliver promised.

Juliet waited, shifting from foot to foot, and tugging her navy blue jacket tightly around her to protect from the blustering wind. The storm was closing in fast. A gust caused the Union Jack on the pole in the center of the square to flap loudly, and sent somebody's straw hat soaring into the air. A moment later, she saw a tourist in cream pants and a blue jacket, dashing across the cobbles in its pursuit.

And then, a sleek Jaguar in racing green, old but well cared for, pulled up alongside her. Oliver was at the wheel, dressed in a plaid shirt and a waterproof jacket, with an anxious expression on his face.

"Juliet. What's going on?" he asked as she scrambled inside and closed the door.

"I've solved the case!" she said. "I think, anyway."

"Who's the killer?" Oliver's eyebrows rose. "This is incredible. You've done all this in a day, while I was out inspecting a historic building? Or rather, what's left of one?"

"We need to move fast," Juliet insisted. "Because I figured out who the killer has to be, and who's been stealing these books. It's the housekeeper! Ellie Edmund."

"Ellie Edmund? The housekeeper?" Oliver echoed in surprise.

"Yes. It has to be her. Alfred knew about the book thefts, and he was doing research to try to find who was stealing them and replacing them with fakes," Juliet explained, as Oliver turned the car and set off, back the way he'd come, heading off the town's main road and up into the hills.

"So you think the housekeeper found out?"

“Yes. She must have done, and decided to kill him, after having stolen one last book.”

“And who was she selling them to?” Oliver asked, as the car headed up the winding road.

“Maybe she found a buyer herself, or advertised online, or even got approached by someone. I’m sure must all have been kept anonymous, with cut-outs and burner phones. I mean, these are very valuable books.”

“What a shock. Imagine a trusted employee turning bad like that. So, how are you going to prove it to the police if it's all been so anonymously done?" he asked.

“The journal, where Alfred wrote down all his suspicions, is in the library. I – um – happened to find it earlier.”

“You did?” Surprise was in Oliver’s voice.

"But the housekeeper might have been searching for it. She might already know where it is and be planning to take it with her. It's evidence, Oliver. Very important evidence. It gives the dates that Alfred was away. And on those dates, the housekeeper posted books from the local post office. I’ve just been there, checking.”

“What amazing work,” he said, as they veered into Alfred’s road. “I’m so impressed that you figured this all out. And I’m glad that you asked me to come with you. This could get dangerous, Juliet!”

“Yes,” she agreed. “I wasn’t too keen to go on my own. But with you, I feel ready for anything!”

Was it her imagination, or did Oliver look slightly alarmed by that, as he steered his Jaguar around the bend.

But then, he braked, hard.

In front of the gate, was a sight she’d never imagined.

Two police cars were parked there, one at an angle with lights flashing. The home’s front door was open wide. And, as Juliet stared in astonishment, she saw three figures appearing.

On the left was Inspector Tennyson. On the right was Constable Coleridge.

And in the middle, with handcuffs around her wrists and one policeman grasping each of her arms, was the housekeeper herself.

Ellie Edmund’s face was sheet white. She was breathing hard as she stumbled along, bracketed by the officers of the law. Behind them strode Basil Douglas, with a hard, set expression on his face.

Watching this play out, Juliet was hyperventilating too. This was an astonishing twist. It seemed that the police had figured it out. How had they done it?

She buzzed down the window, wondering if she could overhear what they were saying. The answer was yes. It was a situation fraught with tension. Everyone was shouting, and the gusting wind was blowing the words her way.

"Miss Edmund, we have evidence that you have been stealing books from your employer, and that yesterday, you stole the auctioned copy of Oliver Twist, and murdered him!" Inspector Tennyson's voice rang out.

"It wasn't me who killed him! Please, believe me!" Ellie's voice was shaking. If the policemen hadn't been holding her arms, Juliet thought she would have collapsed onto the paved pathway. "It wasn't me! I never killed him! It was my afternoon off!"

"It was your afternoon off, so you came back to kill him!" Inspector Tennyson accused.

"Exactly!" Constable Coleridge's single shouted word split the air like a thunderbolt.

Then, Juliet's eyes widened as she saw what Basil Douglas was holding in his hand. It was the journal!

"I just found this under a seat cushion!" he shouted. "It proves beyond any doubt that you were stealing from my brother, who so generously paid your wages, and that he'd just figured out it was you! My brother was going to call the police, and you knew it. You hoped you'd get off scot-free!"

Ellie shook her head violently as she stumbled down to the car, but worse was to come.

"We found a piece of steel piping hidden in the grass outside your room! The murder weapon itself! Forensics will confirm the DNA match!" Inspector Tennyson's voice was sharp. "You'll need to tell us where the book is, though. What did you do with it?"

"I didn't do anything with it! What book?"

"You stole it, didn't you?" Basil accused.

"No!" Tears were streaming from Ellie Edmund's eyes, and her expression was contorted in anguish. Even though Juliet knew she was a thief, who'd killed in anger, in order to conceal her wrongdoings, she couldn't help feeling sorry for her. She was sure if Ellie had known this would be the outcome, the wretched woman would have done a lot of things differently.

"Please, no! I admit to the theft. I – I was tempted into it. I was offered money to send the books to a Mr. Smith. It wasn't my idea! I just went along with it because – because I was being paid such a low wage, and the money was good. But murder? No! Why would I do that? No!"

"We'll take an official statement from you at the police station," Inspector Tennyson said, assisting the sobbing woman into the second police car. "Come with us to the police station, please, sir," he said, turning to Basil. "We'll need to take a statement from you, and also take that book into evidence."

A minute later, the second police car headed off, going slowly down the hill.

Inspector Tennyson and Constable Coleridge got into the other car and set off, lights still flashing. And Basil jumped into his Range Rover and drove off, bringing up the rear.

Juliet stared at the empty street, taking in the drama that had just unfolded before their eyes.

Then, she hastily closed the window as a blast of wind gusted in, bringing the first drops of rain.

"That was – well, that was rather dramatic," Oliver said.

"It was, wasn't it?" Juliet stared at the windshield, now spattered with rain, processing what she'd just heard.

She glanced at Oliver. Oliver glanced at her.

"I guess this lets you off the hook," he said. "That might have been – well, difficult to watch, but at least the killer's in custody now."

"Yes, I suppose I am cleared now," Juliet said. She wished she felt better about it. She couldn't stop thinking of what had happened and the misery and panic in Ellie's voice. The way she'd protested that she was innocent of the killing, while admitting the part she'd played in the thefts.

Wouldn't a killer have denied everything?

"It's odd that she didn't claim to be totally innocent," Juliet said, feeling dizzy by the speed with which her doubts were flooding in.

"Yes, but it might have been a clever ploy," Oliver said. "Admitting to something small makes you look innocent, right?"

"And why would she have left the murder weapon outside her room?" Juliet asked thoughtfully. "Especially if she's so clever, why do that? There were a thousand places she could have put it. She could even have buried it!"

“That did strike me as odd,” Oliver admitted. He straightened his shoulders, turning to her with a serious expression as the rain lashed against the glass and the wind battered the car. “But if she’s not the guilty person, then who is? Just five minutes ago, you were convinced she was guilty, and so was I. Maybe we’re both just second-guessing ourselves.”

But now, the puzzle pieces were rearranging themselves in Juliet’s mind. She’d thought they’d all been perfectly in place. But now she saw that some of them had been misaligned. There was a gap. And there was only one piece that could possibly fill that gap. As she realized the truth, she gasped.

“It’s Basil!” she said.

“What?” Oliver’s eyebrows shot up. “But he had that book with him, waving it around, claiming it was the evidence against Ellie!”

“The book didn’t say that. Alfred wrote that he was going to speak to Basil. Then he wrote that he’d found out who the thief was. And he was right. The thief was Ellie. But she was sending the books to Basil! He was the one who was paying her to steal them and replacing them with cheap fakes. He had it all worked out. That’s why he wasn’t as poor as I expected him to be. When I was listening to the argument between Alfred and Geraldine, Alfred said in an insulting way that Basil didn’t have a penny to his name. But he's driving a very nice car and wearing expensive clothes. He's been making money from this without letting Ellie know who he really is. The parcels were sent to Doncaster. That’s what the post office assistant told me. And Basil lives in Doncaster!”

Realization was now washing over her. Everything made sense.

“So, when Alfred realized that it was Ellie stealing the books, he told Basil, and Basil must have known that it was all over?” Oliver said.

“Exactly,” Juliet replied. “If Alfred got Ellie arrested, then there’d be no more books coming his way. Worse still, the police might follow the trail. Basil had to move fast. And he did. He stole the sought-after Charles Dickens, and then he walked into the house at a time when he knew that Ellie wouldn’t be there. He killed his brother, making sure to plant the murder weapon somewhere it would incriminate Ellie.”

She and Oliver stared at each other. Both were now breathing hard.

“There’s a big problem here, Juliet,” Olier said.

"What's that?" Chills cascaded down her spine. She didn't need a big problem now. They didn't need any problems. A woman was about to be unfairly accused of murder!

"The problem is that we have a great theory. But it can't be proved. There's nothing linking the murders to him. We have no hard evidence."

"Oh, yes, we do," Juliet said automatically, wedded to her theory.

"Really? What is it then?" Oliver asked.

She paused, frowning. "Okay, I revise that. We don't." As she reran the facts in her mind, she realized that Oliver was, unfortunately, right. "We don't have any proof, unless Oliver left his fingerprints on that piece of piping."

"I'm rather convinced he would have worn gloves," Oliver said.

"Me, too," Juliet admitted. She shook her head. "The timing sucks. I mean, if I'd been a minute earlier, I might have seen him leaving!"

"Look on the bright side," Oliver encouraged. "If you'd been a minute earlier, you might also have been hit over the head with a piece of lead piping."

"True," she said, grimacing at the thought.

There was silence in the car.

"Maybe the police will reach the right conclusion, somehow?" Oliver offered hopefully.

But Juliet shook her head. "I don't think that Inspector Tennyson is an expert on the right conclusion."

Frowning, Oliver nodded. "Parking tickets and speeding fines seem to be more his specialty. But how are we going to make things right?"

The events of yesterday were replaying themselves in Juliet's mind. Her walk up the hill. Pausing, surveying the scenery. And finally, proceeding to Alfred's front door, believing she was about to learn more about fake rare books.

Suddenly, an idea leaped into her mind, as she remembered what, exactly, she'd been doing before knocking on that front door.

Juliet grabbed her phone.

"Oliver!" she said. "I might just have found the answer!"

CHAPTER TWENTY THREE

Everything rested on the next few minutes. Juliet felt breathless as the Jaguar reversed into the closest parking place to the police station.

"Ready?" Oliver asked her.

"Ready!" she replied.

"One, two, three!"

Wrenching open the car door, Juliet scrambled out, buffeted by the blowing rain. Quickly, she slammed the door and sprinted for the police station, a gust of water blinding her as her foot splashed into a puddle.

And then, dripping and breathless, they were crowding into the lobby, with Juliet frantically hoping they would be in time.

"Is Inspector Tennyson here?" Juliet asked the officer at the desk, who was now eyeing them both with deep suspicion.

"He's in the back office, processing a suspect and taking a statement."

"Call him!" Juliet demanded. "Immediately! It's urgent. In fact, it's an emergency."

The officer looked as if he was about to argue back, but then Juliet thought he might have seen the expression in her eyes.

"I'll call him," he said, in a voice that contained more respect than she'd yet heard from him.

But then, disaster struck. They heard the tramp of footsteps from the corridor, and Basil Douglas emerged.

He had a smug look on his face and was walking purposefully toward the door. Clearly, he'd given his statement fast, and was now heading out.

Juliet cast a pleading glance at Oliver. If anyone could save the day, it was him.

"Ah, Mr. Douglas," Oliver said, stepping forward and blocking his way. "I've been meaning to speak to you. What a coincidence you're here now. I wanted to ask you if you knew your brother's house might intersect with an old Roman road?"

Basil blinked, as if he was trying to understand this odd question, and work out what it might mean.

"A Roman road?" he asked in surprise.

The delay caused by that moment of confusion was enough. The connecting door opened again, and this time, Inspector Tennyson bustled out, with Constable Coleridge, tall and silent, bringing up the rear.

The inspector stared from Juliet to Oliver and back again.

"I understand you wanted to see me?" he asked. "What's this all about, then?"

“Please,” Juliet said, pointing to Basil, “detain this man. We have evidence that he’s the killer!”

There was a resounding silence for a moment.

Inspector Tennyson looked at Juliet in surprise. Constable Coleridge’s eyebrows rose all the way to the brim of his helmet. And out of the corner of her eye, Juliet saw Basil Douglas tense.

“What on earth are you talking about?” Basil asked incredulously. “I know nothing about this! And you don’t have any proof. You’re just – you’re just attention seeking!”

“I am not attention seeking,” Juliet said calmly. “And I do have proof.”

“What proof do you have?” Inspector Tennyson challenged.

“Well, as I told you, I arrived at the house very shortly after Alfred Douglas was murdered,” Juliet said.

“Yes, but you told me you saw nobody,” Inspector Tennyson reminded her, as Basil nodded enthusiastically.

“I thought I saw nobody. But before I knocked on the door, I saw a message from my sister, back in San Francisco, reminding me to take photos and send them to her. So, I did just that,” Juliet explained.

Inspector Tennyson was looking interested, and Basil was now looking paler than he had done.

“What did the photos capture?” Tennyson asked.

“Let me show you.” Juliet opened her phone and turned the screen. Everybody crowded around.

“This is the first photo. Pure landscape. Quite beautiful,” she said. “Here’s photos number two, three and four. More of the same. Gorgeous early fall colors.”

“Magnificent!” That barked word erupted from Constable Coleridge’s mouth. Everyone jumped in surprise, including him.

But now, Basil was turning to her angrily.

“You really think we have time to watch your vacation slideshow? I have to be back in Doncaster this evening, and have to get on the road. Admit you’re just seeking attention!”

Ignoring him, Juliet turned to the next photo.

"This one is the interesting one. You can see something here. I'm going to enlarge it so you can have a look. It's the corner of a deerstalker hat. In the very background, you can also see a tan shape that resembles a Land Rover. It's parked well down the hill. It's obvious you were walking back to it."

She looked meaningfully at Basil, who raised a guilty hand to his head.

"The colors are identical. And now, we move on to the next one!"

"Wait!" The hoarse word came out in a shout. Sheet-white, Basil's eyes were wide. "Those photos are fabricated, they're nothing but nonsense. You'll never link me to this crime! My brother deserved everything he got! The selfish, self-centered, greedy, arrogant swine! If I hadn't killed him, somebody else would!"

Juliet gasped. They had a confession. She'd never believed it would happen, and it had! In front of the police, right there in the Whistling Willow police station.

For a moment, it seemed as if time had stopped. Nobody moved a muscle. And then, as Inspector Tennyson moved toward Basil, he jumped aside, shouting out words in a voice thrumming with stress.

"You'll never get me! Never! I'm going to make sure those photos never see the light of day!"

And the next moment, he grabbed Juliet's phone right out of her hand, and bolted for the police station door.

"No! My phone!" Juliet shouted. She hadn't backed up to the cloud. There were at least a hundred photos there she didn't want to lose, and several magnificent shots she hadn't had time to send to Sarah.

"My evidence!" Inspector Tennyson yelled, and that drove home the seriousness of the situation.

They all rushed for the door, with Oliver and Inspector Tennyson reaching it together. Constable Coleridge was hot on their heels, and Juliet was racing behind.

"Which way did he go?" Inspector Tennyson shouted as he burst through.

"Left!" Oliver yelled.

"Right!" Constable Coleridge shouted simultaneously.

After the briefest of pauses, Inspector Tennyson veered to the right, racing out into the pouring rain. Oliver turned left, and Juliet pounded behind him. They had to cover all bases. There was no predicting where Basil could have gone. In this weather, his direction was nothing more than a guess. All she knew was that he wasn't in his car. It was parked two spaces away from Oliver's, so she could be sure of that.

The problem was that in this weather, everyone was fleeing. It wasn't like Basil was standing out. The hourly bus had just pulled up, and at least ten people were sprinting through the rain, scurrying in different directions.

He was tall, and he was broad shouldered, and he'd been wearing a tan jacket, expensive looking, with a discreet designer label on it. None of that exactly made him easy to spot, but at least she had guidelines in her mind for looking.

Her phone! Would he keep it with him? Was he planning on destroying it? If only she'd backed up her photos. Sarah would be so mad. Never mind that, she'd be mad at herself, too.

Had he gone down this side street? There was a rushing figure there. The jacket was darker, but it might be from the rain. With her heart pounding, Juliet took two steps down the side street before realizing that this man was much shorter and wider than Basil. It wasn't him. Spinning around, she rushed back to the main street, worried that her wrong turn had lost her time she'd never make up. Oliver was now far ahead. Had he seen Basil? He was racing toward the small park that bordered the main road, as if he had a target to catch up with.

She wanted so badly to help him, but she knew she'd never be fast enough to catch up. Oliver was putting everything into this chase.

So, what could she do then?

She could make sure he hadn't escaped anywhere else. If he'd been sneaky, and ducked away into a shop, or behind a parked car, Oliver might not have seen him in this rain. As the backup person, following behind, that might be a useful thing for her to do.

Scary. And definitely, something that was going to get her very drenched, very soon.

But useful. It might help find Basil if he was hiding, and so far, Basil had proven to be very sneaky. He could be under this parked car, right here.

Nope. Nothing there. But how about hiding in the clothing shop opposite? He could have veered into there and gone to ground behind the rails of jackets and pants, all the new, heavy winter stock already in the shop for the season ahead.

Heading through the door, she heard the bell jingle.

"Can I help you?" the store attendant asked.

Down one aisle, up the next. A peek behind the change room curtain – just in case.

"Hey!" an outraged male voice said, but those legs were way too suntanned to belong to the sallow-skinned Basil.

"Just looking!" she called, barging out of the store and heading down the road again. Oliver was almost out of sight, and she still had no idea where Basil was. Or, where her phone was! This was a serious emergency.

Hold on. Maybe there was a way to solve it. At any rate, what she did might give someone, one of the three other pursuers, a lead.

She ducked back into the clothing store again.

"I'm so sorry," she said. She and the assistant hadn't gotten off to a good start. There was not exactly an atmosphere of trust between them. The young, dark haired woman, in stylish jeans and a sleeveless vest, was staring at her warily, as if wondering what on earth she was going to do now.

"Your phone. Could I possibly borrow it? It's a huge emergency, and I need to make a call," she said.

"No!" That was a pretty reflexive refusal.

"Please?" Juliet begged.

"I don't have any airtime!"

Translating frantically in her head, she realized that meant the store assistant didn't have any minutes. So she couldn't call from her own phone.

She was about to leave the store, when the man from the change room burst out, with two pairs of jeans folded over his arms, wearing blue boxer shorts with yellow ducks on them. He shoved his phone into her hand.

"If it's an emergency, use mine," he said.

"Oh, thank you so much! Thank you!"

As fast as she could, Juliet dialed her own number. Then, she stepped outside. The rain was still falling hard, but the wind had dropped. As she waited for the call to connect, she stared around. She had a loud ringtone. Hopefully, it would be audible to somebody – to Inspector Tennyson, or Constable Coleridge, or even to Oliver.

She waited, breathing hard, peering in every direction through the rain.

And then, from twenty yards up the road, she saw a figure burst out of a gap between two parked cars.

It was him! That tan jacket fit him well, even though the rain had darkened it. And that gray deerstalker had a very conspicuous shape to it.

“Oliver!” she yelled.

She didn’t know if he would hear her in this downpour, but Juliet was surprised by the volume of her own voice. For a librarian who spoke in a voice close to a murmur most times, and who’s most commonly used word was ‘Sssh’, she had hidden depths. Or rather, hidden decibels. Her voice reverberated off the cobbled buildings, and pierced through the falling rain, and ahead, Oliver swung around. He’d heard it.

And, seeing the fleeing man duck down a cobbled alleyway, he raced in pursuit.

“Thank you!” she said, pressing the phone back into the hands of the kind shopper.

And then, she was off. Her phone was still intact, and if she reached it in time, then maybe he wouldn’t have time to smash it.

Oliver was closing in at a fast, purposeful run.

He might need help!

Juliet pounded up the road, aiming for the alleyway, her breath coming fast. She wasn’t used to running. Her chest was burning, and her legs felt as if she’d had ten pounds of lead added to the sole of each shoe. She was really more of a walker. Truth be told, she didn’t even go to the gym as often as she should. But now, everything was at stake. Starting with a killer’s capture and ending with her photo gallery.

So, tough as it was, she forced her legs into a run. Swerving around two women holding large, red umbrellas, she ducked down the alleyway.

Oliver was gaining, or maybe it was just that Basil also wasn’t much of a runner. But, as Juliet toiled up the surprisingly steep alleyway, she saw that Oliver had reached the other man.

He grasped hold of his arm.

"I think that's enough, sir," he gasped out, holding tight to Basil's forearm. Would he fight or struggle? Juliet watched anxiously as she rushed up, knowing that if he did struggle, she'd have to try to intervene. Which would be the best part of him to grab, she wondered. She wasn't very experienced in fights.

But it seemed there was no fight left in the exhausted Basil. He’d run himself into the ground. Bending over, he uttered wheezing gasps as he tried to replenish the air he’d lost in that furious pursuit.

His arm slumped down, and her phone dropped out of his exhausted fingers.

Juliet managed to catch it just before it clattered down onto the cobblestones.

They'd caught a killer. And from behind her, the double set of approaching footsteps signaled that the law was on the scene.

CHAPTER TWENTY FOUR

"But Juliet! I can't believe you didn't tell me any of this!"

Sitting cross-legged on her bed, and wrapped in her toweling robe, Juliet reached out and stroked Gingerbread's fur, listening to his rumbling purr in response.

On the dressing table, in a plastic bag, was her old book. The police had given it back, and luckily, it wasn't too dusty. A good massage with a towel and the fingerprint dust was gone.

"There wasn't really time to tell you everything," she admitted.

"Not time?" Sarah's voice rose incredulously. "There wasn't time to tell me that you were – you were accused of a murder, and had to clear your name, and went around asking questions to people who could actually have been the killer? In fact, you even spoke to the killer himself?"

"Yes, that's how it worked out. And luckily, it all did work out."

"If I'd known, I'd have dropped everything! I'd have taken the next flight over and helped you out! You were in danger, sis. Danger!"

"I would never have asked you to put yourself in danger!" Juliet said. "And to be honest, it was your pics, or rather, the ones I took for you, that saved the day."

"Yes, that's something, at least." Sarah sighed. Then there was a slurping noise. "That was me, finishing up a milkshake," she said.

"Healthy breakfast choice?" Juliet asked quizzically.

"Breakfast of champions," Sarah countered. "But you should be ready for dinner there, right? This time difference is still so confusing. It's strange to think there is such a gap when we talk to each other."

"I know. And yes, you're right. I am going out to dinner."

Maybe it was the way she said the words, or maybe it was just her sister's infallible instinct. But Sarah instantly homed in on what she'd said.

"Alone?" she asked meaningfully. "Or with someone?"

"With a friend," Juliet said. She was not going to say anything further right now. That was all Oliver was. A friend. But she was looking forward to dinner… a lot.

"I'm not accepting that as an explanation," Sarah said.

"It's all the explanation I'm giving you." Juliet stroked Gingerbread's head again, feeling sad that such a friendly cat couldn't live permanently in a guesthouse. She was worried for Ginger's future, even if he seemed entirely contented in his present. "Go look at your pics," she said to Sarah.

"Well, I'm looking at them. But the strange thing is that I can't seem to find the one you said you were going to show that killer before he broke and ran. There's one where you definitely can see the edge of a hat, but it's very far away. And a sliver of car, way in the distance. From what you said, there was supposed to be a clearer one?"

Juliet grinned. "There was no clearer one. It was a bluff."

"What?" Sarah's voice hit a high note usually reserved for opera singers. "A bluff? You bluffed a killer, staring him in the eye, in front of him and the police?"

"Well, it was all I could do. I hoped that he would think it was coming, and admit to his own guilt." Those moments had seemed like an eternity. Juliet wasn't sure how she'd held her nerve. The shy librarian she was, had seemed very far away in that instant. And she'd managed it. He'd broken and then grabbed her phone after gabbling out a confession.

"Wow." Sarah's voice was full of admiration. "Just wow. You know, you've given me an idea."

"About what?" Juliet asked. Switching her phone to speaker, she got off the bed. It was time to start getting ready. She could get changed, and put her make-up on, while she talked.

"An idea for my book, of course. You know, I feel that a romance, with a dash of mystery, is exactly the book I've always wanted to write, sis. The mystery was the missing element I've needed. You and your photos have inspired me. This time, I promise you, I'm going to finish it."

"I hope you do," Juliet smiled, because I want to read it."

She hung up, smiling.

Talking to her sister was so great. Being in the same time zone as her again would make the trip back, in a week and a half's time, feel less final.

Was it normal to feel so bereft at the thought of going back home? California was home, after all. She had her job to look forward to, even though she had been thinking for a while it was becoming boring and she was stuck there. She'd have to find another apartment and a new place to stay.

If only… if only she could have the chance of following her dream. In just a few short days, this beautiful town had begun to feel like a place where her heart could be happy.

How real it had seemed, as she'd sat opposite Mr. Banks, and asked about that teeny tiny retail spot. How she'd longed for her fictitious excuse to be true.

It wasn't though, so she should put it aside. Maybe one day, but not now. Now, she needed to get dressed, ready for her dinner with Oliver. And tomorrow, she could head to the tearoom and tell Amy all about what LA was like.

Enjoy your vacation while it lasts, she thought. It's a week and a half, so every moment is precious. And there might even be more surprises in store. The last couple of days had taught her that you never knew what was around the corner.

Just as she had that thought, her phone started ringing again. This time, her stomach curdled as she saw it was her divorce lawyer on the line.

She hoped this wasn't going to be bad news.

CHAPTER TWENTY FIVE

The small restaurant smelled deliciously of garlic and herbs, and today, the fragrant richness of roast chicken wafted out of the open door. The manager gave her a hopeful glance, but Juliet walked on.

It was eleven thirty a.m., and while the restaurant was preparing for lunch, Juliet was bracing herself for the climb up the stairs, to the estate agent's office above.

It was her sixth day of vacation. And Juliet had an important meeting there.

She didn't feel as if she walked up the stairs. It felt more as if the mix of nerves and excitement inside her wafted her to the upper floor like a balloon on the wind.

Stopping at the top, she took a deep breath. She looked down, startled by the way the sunlight from the gap in the buildings reflected off the gorgeously bright trim of her green jacket. Every time she saw that brightness, she caught her breath. This was the first time she'd worn it. Maybe she'd get used to it after a while. For now, it startled her every time.

Mr. Banks was waiting in his small office at the top of the stairs. Charm itself, he greeted her as if she were a long lost friend.

"Ms. Page! How good to see you on this lovely, fine day, and what a beautiful jacket you're wearing, so flattering to your coloring. It's a true Indian summer day, isn't it? One of the last sunshine days before autumn sets in, or should I say, fall?" He gave her a conspiratorial grin as he ushered her into the room.

"Good to see you, Mr. Banks," she replied.

"I must compliment you on your ingenuity in catching the killer. You know, the whole town is talking about it. It was a worrying time for me, I must say. With an unsolved crime so serious, property values were looking shaky. Now, confidence is soaring again. But what can I do for you?"

She gulped. This meant a lot. Everything, in fact. It was a huge gamble, but she was going to take it.

"You mentioned that you had a retail space open. Is it still available?"

His eyebrows rose. “That space? Yes, it is still available. But are you a serious renter? Forgive me if I seem forward, but my impression was that you were here on vacation. You know, if I'm going to a client, I want to be sure there's a serious offer on the table.”

She was sure that the unspoken question was also whether she could afford the rental, and the costs of opening a new business.

“I’m looking at making a new start.” Deciding to explain more about her circumstance, she continued. “I’m getting divorced.”

“Sorry to hear that,” he murmured, as she continued.

“My husband and I are selling our apartment, which we jointly owned.” She’d always resented those oppressively high payments toward the mortgage. Turns out they were a blessing in disguise. “Our apartment value has skyrocketed since we bought it. The area became very sought after. So, I have a sum of money that I can use to start a business. I even have a small stock of rare books to begin trading."

And that was due to Geraldine’s kindness. On having heard that Juliet had solved the crime, and put her uncle Basil behind bars, she’d gotten hold of her. Even though she and her father had been estranged, he’d never changed his will. She’d invited Juliet to take her pick of Alfred’s stock before she sold the rest.

A shelf of beautifully kept collector’s books now awaited her. The start of her dream.

"I must look into your shop!" Enthusiasm bubbled from Banks' voice. "I've been looking for a couple of specific items and would love to see what's there."

“Maybe you can be my first customer,” she smiled. “Obviously there are still a few legalities to sort out for me as a business owner, getting the correct visas and so on. I’m busy with that, but my lawyer says there shouldn’t be a problem.”

She was very grateful for her law school friend, Jackson. He was a genius! It seemed there was nothing he couldn't do if he set his mind to it.

“Well, that is wonderful. What a stroke of good fortune,” Banks enthused. “As it happens, that retail space is still available. Will you be wanting the upstairs residential space as well? It’s bigger than the shop, though not by much, but it has all the amenities you’ll need.”

“Yes, I will want that.”

Shoebox sized it might be, but the view over the town was glorious, and the apartment had enough space for a bedroom, a bathroom, and a combined living room and kitchen. It had everything she needed. Or should she say, everything she and Gingerbread needed. If she got this place, then the cat was moving in with her, she decided.

He passed a few papers across the desk, the pages thick and glossy and blinding white.

"Just sign here, and here, and here. And we can start the process."

Excitement filled her. She couldn't wait to tell Sarah about this. And she knew Oliver would be as happy as she was about this move, even though she felt unsure about telling him. Telling him felt like a commitment. But that was a worry for the future.

As she put the pen down, Banks' hand reached out to hers, and he shook it firmly.

"Welcome to Whistling Willow, Ms. Page. I hope you, and your business, will have many happy years ahead."

NOW AVAILABLE!

BOUND FOR MURDER: A LETHAL LEXICON
(A Juliet Page Cozy Mystery—Book 2)

Librarian Juliet Page decides to pursue her dream, and to restart her life in a small town in the UK, and open her own rare bookshop. But the grand opening of her bookstore takes a dark turn when a rare book sale ends in murder--and she's the prime suspect. Can she decipher the clues hidden in the dusty pages and clear her name before it's too late?

BOUND FOR MURDER: A LETHAL LEXICON (A Juliet Page Cozy Mystery—Book 2) is the second novel in a new series by cozy mystery author Audrey Shine. The series begins with BOUND FOR MURDER: A HARDCOVER HOMICIDE (Book 1).

A charming cozy mystery series, Juliet Page will pull you right into its quaint setting, captivate you with its enchanting atmosphere, and make it impossible to stop reading. With unexpected plot twists and a perplexing mystery to unravel, this page-turner will keep you engaged late into the night, all while you fall in love with its unforgettable main character.

Future books in the series are also available!

Audrey Shine

Audrey Shine is author of the JULIET PAGE COZY MYSTERY series, comprising five books (and counting).

Audrey would love to hear from you, so please visit www.audreyshineauthor.com to receive free ebooks, hear the latest news, and stay in touch.

BOOKS BY AUDREY SHINE

JULIET PAGE COZY MYSTERY
A HARDCOVER HOMICIDE (Book #1)
A LETHAL LEXICON (Book #2)
A VOLUME IN VENGEANCE (Book #3)
A TYPESET TRAGEDY (Book #4)
A FATAL FOOTNOTE (Book #5)

Made in United States
Troutdale, OR
04/18/2025